CW00503209

Adorable

"Ida Marie Hede's *Adorable* is this incredible, tiny, undead person you can possess and make mouth subconscious astonishments. The transubstantiation of book to wet undead joy comes from Hede's use of words for feelings and experiences fantastically resistant to representation. In its vivid wrangle, Hede's language blooms into dazzling gratuity by anaphoric increments, as it laps hungrily at death and toddlers and shit and grief and slime and herself. The whole thing glistens and then spontaneously incorporates."
— Ed Atkins

"A teeming, fluid book wet with leaking bodies, influences, concerns, memories, moods. Hede's defamiliarising creation brims over with love and broaches our consciousness, making our own world hot and sticky. Viscerally apt reading for the fraught era we find ourselves in: obsessed with contagion and encroachment, yet besotted with connection and touch."
— Jen Calleja

"*Adorable* pulls us between wanting to live and having to die, between child found and parent lost, feeling from inside Hede's brain-womb all that hide and seek within the concaves of living rooms, telephone calls, and other skins. An urgent, brutally tactile novel that grows boundless in the mind, *Adorable* achieves life."
— Mara Coson

"Ida Marie Hede writes about the trivialities of life and death with a swirling and bubbling and completely shameless brilliance that this reader just cannot get enough of."
— Lars Bukdahl, *Weekendavisen*

Adorable

Ida Marie Hede

Translated from the Danish
by Sherilyn Nicolette Hellberg

Lolli Editions

1.
A HEART-SHAPED
BUM

B IS A GROWN woman, she has a rhombus-shaped bum.

Q is a grown man, he has a square bum.

Æ is small.

Her bum is heart-shaped.

Compared to ants, beetles and flower pistils, Æ is a giant.

From the perspective of a human — from a B perspective, a Q perspective — Æ is absolutely miniature.

She laughs and pushes open a door. She wobbles into their empty bedroom. She hides behind a curtain, in a room of hefty feelings. A recent argument hangs limply in the white material. Then she walks into the hallway, down the stairs, it's dark. Her face in a spider web. A spider web across her cheeks. She goes outside. A woodlouse between the bricks in the driveway. She stumbles, she spins around, she's still tangled in the spider web. A lace veil over her mouth. A small fly on a spider web thread goes right down her throat. Into her stomach, where it sputters. Fly wings in a still-growing stomach.

On the idyllic suburban street, where spring is on full display, there are white-painted houses, driveways, large gardens with trampolines and fruit trees. There is shit from the snails, from the compost and the cats' paws.

The idyllic suburban street doesn't have a bum, but if it did, it would be a round and bulging one.

Stuffed almost.

Nørreport's bum is different. It's just okay — speckled by heat discoloration, uneven around the edges, like it's been poorly Photoshopped.

Nørreport is disgusting in its own way. Secretions from countless living things seem especially uncomfortable here, lazier, squished around the kerbs, in the cracks between the slabs of concrete, dog shit and spit and ketchup. It can't just slide into the ground. It has to sparkle in its foulness. And then there's everything else, flapping plastic bags and blue shards of glass and balloon knots. But all of this human detritus doesn't have any bacteria inside it. Nørreport's walls and asphalt don't have enough foreign bodies to make living bodies immune: a body needs to encounter new bacteria every day in a varied stream. That's how the body develops its protection. That's how the body stays alive. That's how human survival is ensured.

B and Q take Æ and roll her across the floor of the metro towards Nørreport.

Æ rolls like a little bundle.

Or like a snail, slow.

None of the other passengers pick her up.

Or give her a push.

She's not their child, they probably don't dare.

What, would you grab the neck of her sweater or one of her pigtails or something.

Grab her wrist.

The trail of slime behind Æ is made of spit, flakes of skin, sweat.

Hurried finger-doodles on the metro's linoleum floor.
Æ could roll forever.

Roll as far as the train car reaches. Collecting dirt, cigarette stubs, insect wings and bits of liquorice from the floor. Pressing them into the palms of her hands and her bird's nest of hair and her puffy jumpsuit.

Finally coming to a stop by the panoramic window.

Her clothes, smothered with hundreds of small chunks, like sprinkles.

Lying on her belly with her hands folded under her body and her bum in the air and her face pressed flat against the floor.

B'S BELLY IS FLAT NOW. She really loves its doughy flatness. The punctured white softness that will never be tight again.

Before the flatness her belly is temporarily full, absolutely bulging. A piece of skin around something kicking and living, which is Æ.

Æ is pulled out of B's womb with forceps that grab her temples. Small red indents on her temples. Æ comes out coated in bacteria from B's vagina and arse. Bacteria seep into Æ and trigger an immune response: now Æ can live for a thousand years. But it's almost like Æ doesn't want to come out — her head won't turn the last bit of the way in B's pelvis; a head is actually stuck, pushing on her cervix. Warm, drawn-out spasms of pain, and Æ will have to be taken out by C-section.

If Æ comes out through B's sliced-open belly, there won't be enough bacteria. The doctor needs to stick a finger up B's arsehole, rotate it deftly and then smear a wet finger caked with bacteria across Æ's shrieking lips.

It doesn't matter how Æ was born, her lips quickly locate B's nipples and start sucking. Milk and cracked skin, gums gnawing on breast flesh.

B would like to live for a thousand years too. She holds Æ in her arms, Æ is so new. B can barely figure out how to hold her. As long as she doesn't drop her: lose hold of her head and break her neck.

Now that Æ exists, B wants to survive the apocalypse everyone is talking about. She wants to grow old and wrinkled and withered and shrunken so she can stay in the world with Æ. She wants to communicate with an adult Æ on the phones of the future. Maybe through some form of telepathy, maybe through small strands of DNA — conversing with each other as mother and daughter will, in the future that might be.

B no longer doubts the future or its new technologies. Æ's presence moves the lifespan of all things infinitely *outwards*.

B says she wants to be stronger too, to have bacteria from a body that is not her own. Bacteria is like a life-giving elixir: *faecal bacteria from X are transplanted into Y's digestive tract and changes are observed in Y's mood and metabolism.*

Her belly skin is nowhere near tight again, the lacerations on her uterine walls not even slightly healed. B bleeds into her big mum-nappy, long slimy strands.

Maybe she needs to go home and rest, to lie down with her legs up and with Æ balanced on her belly and a croissant in her hand. Æ's mouth on her breast and stiff splashes of milk on her baby face.

Or maybe she's too eager and can't relax. After Æ is born, she can't get enough life. She's taken directly from the delivery room to the gastroenterology ward.

There, a probe is inserted through B's oesophagus and into her stomach. Down here, the party is already in full swing! There are billions of faecal bacteria in B's stomach, more than there are humans on Earth, bacteria that have lived for millions of years, which moved into B the day she was born, and which will move on when she dies. In that sense, the word *human* isn't very accurate. She's not mostly *human*, not at all. Bacteria bounce around, frolicking with half-digested food, as if inside a centrifuge. But it's not enough, she needs more! Inside the tube, there's shit from a shit-donor whom B doesn't know. As the shit descends into her system, B is dangerously close to the brown mass: only the plastic barrier of the probe separates her from the stranger's shit, sliding through her to become part of her intestinal flora.

She might as well have eaten the poo herself.

B is waiting for a change. Bacteria gives everyone a second chance.

So the skinny person can become a chubby person, the aggressive person can become a calm person, the restless one even-keeled, the depressed and anxious person can become optimistic and impulsive, the optimistic and hopeful person can become deadly serious and thereby increase their sex appeal.

And the person who loves long black lace opera gloves and full polka-dot skirts and big white plastic hairclips will want to wear tracksuits and shrunken woollen vests and sexy black baseball caps that make your eyes really round and blue.

And the person who loves T-shirts with bleach stains and pasty everyday faces and post-humanist theory will want to dance the lindy hop, a dance that makes your cheeks rosy-red.

The person in Buffalo boots puts on an old fisherman's sweater, the person with acne gets glowing skin, the person with raised eyebrows can have them lowered, the too-pretty person can get a little more asymmetrical.

The person who's always been missing a crooked and compelling scar on their cheek gets a crooked and compelling scar on their cheek, the person with big boobs gets small boobs, the person with a flowering arm gets a shrivelled arm.

The wildly hairy person loses all their hair, the person who feels too white gets darker skin, the woman who's had multiple abortions loses her ability to conceive, the person with a belly flat like a pancake gets a swollen belly that's doughy like sandwich bread.

So that everyone will be able to achieve their desires, so that all of us, the oppressed, can transform ourselves and become the upstanding humans we all secretly dream of being.

So that all of us, the ones in power, can transform ourselves and become the courageous underdogs we all secretly dream of being, and maybe already are.

Who sent the poo? Just as they're always in the process of producing semen, bodies keep producing shit. If there's a shortage of shit somewhere in the world, more is likely to turn up soon somewhere else.

More babies, better mood, worse smell.

B doesn't know who donated her faecal sample, the hospital won't give her that kind of information. Whether it was a hopeful gift from an old arsehole, *sweetheart, I'm giving you the best-cut stuff I've got.*

B is back home. She watches movies on the couch while she nurses Æ.

In Pasolini's *Salò*, a group of teenagers are held captive in a castle. They're served swollen chunks of shit on porcelain platters and they eat them slowly from porcelain plates, revolted, punctuated by fits of vomiting, down goes the shit.

Æ gurgles, milk spouts out of her and soaks a cloth nappy, a shirt, baby eyelashes, peach fuzz.

FRIDAY NIGHT: B AND Q wipe Æ's bottom with toilet paper and small slippery wet wipes and damp cotton balls. B and Q are on their knees, wiping streaks of shit off the toilet seat and off the walls and off the shower and off the shower curtain and off baby thighs. Æ's baby bum cheeks are swollen and red, shiny and trembling too once the clinging shit splotches have been removed.

B and Q scrape caked shit off her little princess underwear with a spoon. They let the cakes fall into the bin from way too high up: brown-yellow kernels fill the air. Shit kernels splatter their faces, as if the compacted chunks of poo have been vaporised and transformed into an airborne disease or a malignant perfume.

B and Q squeeze their eyes shut and contort their faces, lick something wet off their lips. They taste the squirts of shit. They wash and dry and pour rubbing alcohol over their hands, they can't avoid getting shit all over their hands. They shriek as they watch pruney fingers appear beneath the light brown sludge.

B and Q have taken off Æ's nappy.

Until Æ learns to understand this new situation and can run to the toilet on her own, they'll wipe Æ's pee up from the floor: dark-yellow puddles that turn into streams along the floorboards or hide in overflowing pools behind the toy kitchen and cabinet doors and under deflated balloons in the corners of the living room.

When they find a puddle, an arm of pee has often branched out and taken the shape of: an elephant trunk a prosthesis a curved penis a wing.

Æ's excretions, the deep puddles of pee on the floor, are like tissue she casts off. With each ornamented shit that lands somewhere in the house, by chance shaped like a spinning top, she approaches a new stage of maturity.

B's own age has been fuzzy for a while.

It's mainly through Æ that B feels herself ageing. Æ's growing body takes her by surprise, breaks down her defences: flays the still image she has of herself in a forever-young body. It's not that Æ is growing taller than she is. It's that she's growing at all: that look in her eye. Has that voice, suddenly skinny legs — as if during the night someone gobbled the fat off her baby thighbones, maybe the greedy mouth that lives under the bed but never bothers to chew on B.

Æ has quickly learned how to exist. She's made B's old mannerisms her own. She's taken them without asking and left B newly self-conscious of every raised eyebrow, every nuzzled earlobe.

But there are plenty of mannerisms in the world. Enough for everyone.

Movements aren't like money, aren't like non-perishables, aren't like food, aren't like medicine. No one stockpiles them or hoards them, B thinks.

You can make yourself aware of movements.

B sees herself in Æ.

B gives her movements a little extra edge.

At night, the television running, a shadow game on the wall in the light of the floor lamp: Æ's arms like flapping tree branches, like the chains goth kids wear, like something with a beak or a mouth. Everyone points and jumps with joy. Æ scares herself. She pulls her hands in. How can the body make a shadow, excrete something that appears so sharply? An image that seems delayed at first. The shadow runs after the arm it's attached to like a child running after an adult, but then without warning it catches up to the arm and moves in front of it, wagging almost teasingly, more flapping and elegant, as if it were pointing out the pink porcine arm suspended in the air, *here I am dressed in grey, more precise than you.*

B tries to approach the idea of inevitable disintegration. That she is decay wrapped in skin, like a moist cake wrapped in fondant.

On the outside:

Crème de la mer, irritated hair follicles, sweat smell, Nivea smell, crusted self-tanner, crusted sugar, crusted discharge, cotton undershirt, wool tights, tweed skirt, polyester shirt, wool cardigan, gold jewellery, Jil Sander No. 4, bogeys, scabs, dead hair and living hair and on-its-way-out-of-the-head hair.

On the inside:

A marsh of starving bacteria and snaking organs twisted around each other, turning her body into a lazy swampscape.

The kind of place where you can set little turquoise toy houses on the boggy ground, little doll men and doll women who stay in place for a moment before they start to sink.

The kind of place where an electric light is on in the toy kitchen, but not in the bedroom.

The kind of place where a lamp exhaustedly blinks, the bulb won't go out.

The kind of place where small figures are set in orange beds beneath stiff quilts. A troll behind the toilet bowl.

NEXT TO Æ'S BED ARE small multicoloured lamps. Posters are attached to the sloped ceilings with sticky tack. *Jungle-dyret Hugo* and *Rita the Fox*. The posters are so erratically hung. Maybe they'll fall onto Æ's sleeping body.

B kisses Æ goodnight. It's growling, Æ says, and points at B's fat rolls: the sound of the belly that in a way still belongs to them both. A space for memories of countless episodes.

To Æ, that belly is like an old house: or like a photograph of a childhood home you can point to and tell stories about. In that room, I was conceived; in that room, I was born.

To B, that belly is an incessantly thinking piece of flesh. The millions of neurons in the belly make up a miniature brain, like a cat's brain. That's what Æ grew out of, spun from a cat's thoughts.

Æ thinks:

Mum, you were able to hold me in there: eating, breathing, working, shitting, partying, shouting, thinking with me inside you. I was conscious but without narrative memory. I was just floating around like a lazy snail. I saw out of your belly button. Or: With my X-ray vision that made your skin and flesh disappear, I saw everything. Or: I actually didn't open my eyes at all. My eyelids were thick. They were tucked inside the blanket of your uterus and the transparent fluid I was rolling around in. Or: You didn't know what kind of conscious I was, how much I understood. You didn't know what language to use to describe my swimming movements. You didn't know why I kicked you, causing the jerk in your belly that made you worry your belly skin would pop. If I was trying to get your attention. If I was a little alien with a jagged crown. If I even knew that you existed. You had the sense that I was smarter than you: you had to renegotiate your ideas about what it means to know something. You had to renegotiate your ideas about what life is. Your brain ran faster. In that sense, you sucked something out of me too. You felt humble, but not oppressed. Not weak. Because you had to be strong enough to carry me.

Æ says:

Mum
in your belly, I saw you pick your nose
in your belly, I ate sausages for the first time
in your belly, I lived in London
in your belly, I learned that whales eat Onkel Reje

Intestines jostle: the last sounds before Æ falls asleep.

Still like marzipan. But angular too, as if more bones have emerged. As if the bones inside are fighting for space.

Her skin thicker and more dimpled. Shrunken white stretch-marks draw grooves in her belly fat like ridge-cut crisps. Her belly button hasn't grown larger or smaller, but once in a while it disappears entirely into her white, soft, billowing belly fat; the fold marks a border in the fat and looks like a long surgical scar.

Her armpit skin is brown, the brown can't be scrubbed off, her teeth yellow, the yellow can't be brushed off, the red blood vessels on her cheeks can't be covered by founda-tion. The small whiteheads that appear on her eyelids and around her nostrils can't be popped, they're like enduring monuments.

But B has never been the type to languish.

The anxiety bound to the process of decay has instead be-come an avid interest in the coquettish signs of change.

But.

When it comes to Æ, the slightest transformation comes with a sense of relief.

Something has come full circle.

That's how it is when B looks at Æ:

An unpredictable landscape. Piles of sand soaked by salty

water, the kind of landscape that is pink even in winter.

But not a landscape that you can hold in your hands.

Not a piece of nature.

More an uncharted zone.

A little wobbly, a little tacky, a little chaotic and humid.

A little adorable.

A hot-air balloon hastily dips to lift Æ into its decadent basket, a red race car parks in front of the house, full of immaculately dressed girls from the gymnastics team, who fling their chirping love over Æ.

A bus accelerates, packed with smart outdoorsy children who are going on a trip around the world and are looking for someone like Æ.

Now the kids are coming to pick her up.

But they might not make it.

A tank ploughs into the back garden, brakes so hard it tears up the lawn. Out jumps a pack of screaming charlatans, little boys with Dax Wax in their hair and neckties and pirate swords and snakes and backpacks, a flock of cheeky little guys who get right to work, pitching tents in the garden, tipping grass out of wheelbarrows, unpacking their picnic baskets, building houses in the trees, digging deep and charming holes in the ground, stuffing their tree houses with hot-dog buffets and brambles and fishing poles and dinosaurs, hanging iPads from the branches on metallic ribbons and calling out to Æ.

And Æ, where is she, she's running around down there. Her hair is messy and tangled, she's wearing a flapping set of Hello Kitty clothes covered in faces, as if her own perpetually surprised and inquisitive and eager face has cloned itself, in that way that kids so easily do impossible things: science fiction effortlessly radiates from their fingers. Imaginary but deeply believable creatures materialise in circles around the kids, effortlessly becoming characters in the game's narrative about how people can be together.

She disappears in and out of the depths of the hole, she holds friends' hands like dangling charms, like trusted extensions of herself. The girl with the little scar from a cleft lip and the girl with the spindly legs and almost adult-sized sandals and the girl with the golden blonde hair and the crazy dimples. They run hand-in-hand, she holds onto their fingertips. Through the shrubbery and into the cat's passageway and then they've disappeared.

And then they reappear.

And they're suddenly long-legged and almost unrecognisable aside from the patterns on their dresses, the dresses are still on them, skin-tight and tearing at the seams.

And then the fabric rips open.

And then their bodies are chubby and waddling. Rolls of fat poke through tattered dress shreds.

They reason like adults.

They have political opinions.

They believe, for example, in individual freedom.

They think, maybe:

That you should always repay your debts, no matter the circumstances.

They think, maybe:

That you should be able to take care of yourself no matter how you were raised or registered, no matter what kind of body you have or what kind of brain, or how that body was encountered before there was any chance to object.

They think, maybe:

That you shouldn't be so confrontational, behave so inappropriately, be too reserved or shrill, be too much, you know, too weird, talk back, you know, make odd faces, no matter what kind of body you have or what colour your skin is, or what kind of brain or what kind of desire, no matter how you're met by the world, no matter whether or not you have the right to object.

They think, maybe:

That you should try to work a little structure into your surroundings, you can't just live by your own internal clock, live like a snail, squander your time; they think you should straighten up a bit, conform to the gauzy, natural rhythms of the work day and the work month.

They think, maybe, that it's ridiculous to fall head-over-heels in love or that it's doomed to fail when two people who have different heights or different ages or different nationalities or different ethnicities or different metabolisms or who have the same gender or the same far-reaching problems or the same childhood traumas fall in love and delude themselves into thinking it will make them happy.

They think, maybe, that you can just stay in your own country and try to solve the problems there, that you can try a little harder, it can't be the case that you *have* to run away from everything, you probably just haven't tried hard enough, there must be some other opportunities.

They think, maybe, that you can do what you want, and there are moments when they actually believe that, especially when they're drunk or really high on caffeine or have just finished spring cleaning.

Maybe they like to lie in the grass and nuzzle an ant behind the ears or fantasise about a cat and feel Zen and then the next second they race off in a car and later a plane, endlessly occupied.

Maybe they feel on top after a day of being endlessly occupied, even though they feel terribly exhausted too, it's the eternal struggle, endless Excel spreadsheets, emails, seminar planning, ordering the catering, location scouting, going over blueprints, reading articles, giving feedback, finishing a portfolio, enumerating tasks, presenting a three-month plan and a one-year plan and a five-year plan, coaching, training interns, meetings with the board, orientation for the new Adobe package, trivia at the summer party, periodic reviews from middle management, stocking the breakroom cabinet, munching on marble cake.

Or they feel depleted and burned out after yet another day of actually not doing much besides defining and carrying out their tasks, tasks on their tables thanks to their ambition and hunger and feeling of indispensability, thanks to their brains' unorthodox abilities, and they move sluggishly through those days and then start to accelerate, restless and bitter and drained because their performance can't be measured on any scale, and they can't convince anyone else of their worth, and the reptile brain almost always short-circuits when you can't convince others of your worth.

Or they lie in bed, banging their heads against a pleated lampshade.

Or they furiously pick their noses: oh look, a bit of blood.

Or they watch nine episodes of GoT and throw up on their hairbrushes.

Or they scrub the toilet bowl with Coca-Cola.

Or they post pictures of their lunches on Instagram.

Or they dislodge a piece of food stuck between an incisor and a molar.

Or they eat carrot cake at a café or in the canteen with their mouths open, and it's not very cute.

Or they're annoyed with each other and can't forgive each other.

Then they forgive each other.

But they still talk behind each other's backs, and they feel bad about it, and then they're annoyed about feeling bad about it.

Or they forge alliances and sign contracts with white wine and beer and lip balm and Eight Hour Cream and make doodles and plan weekend getaways in symbiotic bliss.

Or they cry and soak each other's turquoise vintage shirts with mascara tears and give each other money for the dry cleaner.

And then they go out in the garden with coffee and clementines.

They go out in the garden with a cat-o'nine-tails.

They go out in the garden with a handwritten letter from a grandmother.

They go out in the garden with a shabby stuffed robin.

They go out in the garden with a silk-wool scarf that's warm and comforting.

They go out in the garden with a little book about origami and a pair of scissors.

And then they drift off in the grass and sleep in piles.

And look so small.

Curled up, their faces utterly quiet.

They're actually small again.

They're actually still kids.

They're not at all anaemic, not at all long-legged, not at all depraved. They haven't yet become anything at all. They don't have opinions about anything at all: or their opinions are always turning into something else, they're always opening, always doubling, budding or going under.

You can't predict anything about them, they're completely pink, completely crumbly.

They lie in the grass with woodlice on their backs, flies by their noses.

There's something transparent about Æ, as if her skin still isn't thick enough to cover her skull. Especially her eyelids — they're full of blue veins.

And her teeth. They're so white.

A LONG YELLOW TRAIL OF snot dangles from a porcelain nose, swings into her mouth like an acrobat, elegantly it's slurped in, swallowed.

B and Q take her everywhere. She goes to parties and dinners, she goes to the pub, she goes to concerts, artist talks, seminars. She's fat and adorable, little boxing arms, purple onesie, white knitted hat, her face pressed against B's chest.

Æ is sleeping. She lies in the buggy with open, alert eyes, or in a stranger's arms, rocked and whispered to, later drowsy with milk, almost unconscious, but in that way where she can still wake up at any moment, where all attention is therefore always indisputably moving in her direction.

As if she were a little altar, a healing stone or an authority.

She can't say anything but little *growls*, they call it her special language, then slowly she starts to babble out words.

B attends a conference with Æ on her chest and in her arms. B wants to be there. She wants to do everything with Æ and no one is going to tell her that she can't do everything with Æ. No one is going to say the words *hormonal* or *retreating from the world* or *putting life on hold*. No one is going to say that she's not moving. B wants to move, to move with Æ, Æ is an extension of her body, and her body can do anything now that the lesions in her uterus are healed, now that only the one vein on her right labia is still sore, almost always sore, a little monumental ridge you can nudge with an index finger.

B wants to do everything, and B will do everything.

Together with Æ.

The conference is about feminism and the politics of collec-

tive art, and now Tania Bruguera is presenting. As soon as
Æ starts babbling, B and Æ are asked to leave:

Æ's voice will be audible on the conference recording and
they simply can't have that. In the 1970s all the women had
babies on their arms and we can't hear shit of what they said
on the recordings.

Now history is gone (says the persistent woman in the auditorium), what are we supposed to do?

B and Æ leave the auditorium. B thinks about the fleeting
quality of documentation, about recordings of historic conversations drowned out by baby babbles:

Wollt ihr den totalen Krieg drowned out by baby babbles.

Ich bin ein Berliner drowned out by baby babbles.

Marilyn Monroe's Happy birthday to youuuuuu drowned
out by baby babbles.

Donald Trump's American carnage drowned out by baby
babbles.

Drones and fire alarms drowned out by baby babbles.

Coffee makers and rustling satin and mansplaining
drowned out by baby babbles.

Old recordings from London, from Parliament Square, twenty public moments of silence following various tragedies,
where you can hear doves flapping, coughing, phones, car
traffic, drowned out by baby babbles.

Everything that's ever existed as sound waves drowned out by baby babbles.

A miniature memoir from a baby's mouth, finding babbles lurking in a conversation like a tic in the midst of the gravest matters.

Like when Friedrich Jürgenson, the pioneer of *electronic voice phenomena*, leaves his recording device in the garden, maybe placing it under the magnolia tree, maybe placing it in the strawberry patch, he records white noise, he tries to localise the voices of the dead at various frequencies.

Suddenly he hears the voice of his deceased mother there.

He hadn't expected that.

On a recording suddenly hearing either your mother or your child.

Who would you rather hear, do you *have* to choose.

B WRITES EXCLUSIVELY DURING Æ's afternoon naps: she writes for an hour and a half every day from one to two thirty at a café, high on a double espresso or two. She writes that way every day, on that day she writes that everything is ruined, the dollhouse imploded, our tall, shiny wellies got stuck in the swamp.

For B there's always a surprising lag between whatever Æ does and the impulses she suddenly has.

They read a fairy tale, *Mørkebarnet*. Look at my hand! Æ exclaims, the shadow! Right there, Mummy!

It could have been any book.

Æ is restless in a way no adult can afford to be.

Æ can make any adult feel worthless, but immediately afterwards indispensable again.

Æ speaks:

so i have a little brother, i have my little brothers... secret. im inside my little brothers belly, with all the food, and im all squished and chewed up. and then he spits me out, and then he blows into his belly button, and then i get blown up, and then coca-cola comes into my belly button and i get blown up! i love clay, bamse, kylling, ælling, dirt, sky... and my friend... and mummy and daddy and me and å and y and elsa and anna! but not hans! i was born in london, i want to go to potato land, youll die after me, right, mummy? when youre old, i can decide, and i can have sweets because youll be dead. im drawing a big baby with chicken pox. if you die, how will i make breakfast, how will i get to school? do things die, do houses die, do cars die, do they go to the museum, do people go to the museum too, if you die and go to the museum, mummy, can i call you there, if your phone isnt dead too, is it? look im all the way up here, look at me. do teddy bears die?

There's always a surprising lag between the things B does and the series of longings she suddenly feels. A Moroccan rug, the ugliest hair, the idea of an entire day alone, the most gossipy friends, a time machine, a universal credit card to use at ATMs in every city, Æ's arms around her neck in bed at night, a house in the middle of a lake of algae, an explanation for everything, a Whopper in a hotel room all exist inside her simultaneously.

Q HAS BECOME ADDICTED to tattoos, he's always getting more. He has seven now.

What does a good skull look like? he asks. Like in a cartoon?

That one is too plastic, B says.

That one is slanted too much to the right, B says.

That one is cute in a goth way, the eye holes are totally wild!

You should get a huge BONE FACE on your face, like an X-ray on your skin! B says.

Q doesn't listen to her advice.

He's already on his way home with his new tattoo wrapped up in plastic (at first B thinks the plastic is his skin, super-humanly moisturised, all shiny).

At first the tattoo is an open wound. Later the pigment sinks in, the colour disperses under the skin and sets. This time it's like the cream doesn't absorb the same way. Q manically moisturises his arm multiple times a day.

Q says:

When I die these colours will disintegrate like everything else.

Sailors got tattoos so they could be identified if they washed ashore. Maybe after they were disfigured by keelhauling, torn to pieces by the barnacles on the bottom of the ship. Later, they were half degraded by the sea.

Sailors were workers. Assembly line products, like cows. Cows are branded, a way to standardise the individual among the herd.

But cows don't turn their brands into fashion. Cows don't brand each other in elegant colour combinations after they've escaped from the farm, reclining under a tree in the field. They don't bedazzle themselves with neck chains and cowbells. They don't make hats out of milking stools, decorated with lace apron trims. Cows don't reflect on what it means not to be exploited, what it means to be free, what it means to turn a mark of enslavement into an aesthetic.

B thinks that Q gets these tattoos because he loves the ritual stamp, which marks him as both different and belonging. It makes his common human skin special, but also signals that he is engaged with his culture. The tattoo gives him control over the body that feels so comfortably familiar, but still uncontrollable when it suddenly changes, gets heavy or loose, when his muscles suddenly tense. Filling his skin with ink gives him a sense of agency in a world where all forms of intervention escape him.

B imagines a tattoo on her bum cheeks: a pair of arse-cheek curtains.

Drapes covering the bright whiteness.

The tattoo as an article of clothing. A pair of underpants. A warm blanket.

B imagines a tattoo where a hundred rats are eating each other's tails.

A workbook.

A really bad dick.

Three drops of sperm.

Four lazy drops of discharge.

The outline of the egg excreted with her discharge this morning.

An emoji, happy.

An emoji, tears.

An emoji, crazy face.

More emojis, praying hands, clapping hands.

Skulls stacked inside each other, their black outlines like bracelets.

A fly on a dick (at the tattoo parlour it's always free).

A snake on a neck (only tattoo artists have tattooed necks).

A feather, red, slightly faded, like the one B's friend C has. Now it almost looks like a bruise on C's arm: a vein made with the tattoo artist's red carcinogenic cadmium.

No one would be able to identify C's waterlogged body.

But Q, with his eight tattoos, everyone would be able to identify his.

FRIDAY NIGHT: B HAS put Æ down.

Æ is sleeping warmly. Her sweaty fringe is shaped like a miniature cat-o'nine-tails over her temples and forehead.

B and Q, now on the sofa downstairs with cake plates: porcelain platters with racehorses on them. They're tired. Their backs arch and their legs bend feebly. They slowly collapse into each other, lie as curled up as they can. They compete to show each other elegance in their uselessness.

A radio broadcast about animals with infrared vision plays on the computer. The sound is coming from the living room speakers, the TV is on, but muted: the film *Night of the Hunter* from 1955 is playing, with Robert Mitchum as a misogynistic serial killer — you see his hands, covered in tattoos:

One knuckle reads LOVE, the other HATE.

B has read about Harry Dodge, the artist with the words FLOW and FORM tattooed on his knuckles.

You could also write HAIR and SKIN.

B raises her arm:

A lazy Brazilian wandering spider is sitting on the back of her hand, it's come from the bowl of bananas in the kitchen. On its underside a transparent membrane full of eggs ready to burst. The spider takes a slow step with one leg, as if wearing brand-new stilettos and scared it might fall.

It should be scared, it's come to a dangerous place.

B sticks her other hand into her underwear, it itches. The hair on her labia is slightly trimmed. On her legs long, almost twisting hair.

Q has a five-day shadow.

They don't have sex, not tonight on the sofa. They want to get inside each other, but they don't have the energy. They get inside each other in another way, by giving in to the deliciousness of sweat. By imagining their skin as just an inviting layer that needs to be dissolved before a more advanced form of fusion can take place. They work to soften their skin. Scratch it and sand it down. They lie on top of each other with cake and whipped cream in the corners of their mouths, on their cheeks, smeared to their hairlines. The whipped cream is a substitute for sperm, or half-dried white discharge, smeared across their chins and necks and over the tops of their chests: over Q's curly corkscrew chest hair. Over B's wriggling wrinkles that stretch from the breast fat on her neck to her cleavage. They are trying to show each other their devotion. To show each other the exhausted and unkempt and bitter love that they do still have together now that they can't boast a stylish and romantically celebratory deeply eternally hungry love sown with rose petals and tenancy agreements.

B says, your new tattoo is chafing me, I'm getting blisters.

Q says, put a shirt on.

B says, okay.

Q says, the worn light in the living room is winter light, but I'm still sweating like crazy.

B says, it's the cake.

Q says, my "I" today seems to be the usual convergence of bodily discomfort, hunger, news trash, sarcasm and procrastination.

B says, my "I" today seems to be the usual convergence of neurotic itching in my pubic hair, sarcasm, sloppy, unfinished ideas and surrendering to caffeine.

Q says, the only freedom under capitalism is money, freedom understood as liberation from relying on those who won't actually help you in the end, liberation from a feeling of constant humiliation.

B says, money is a consolation for us, but it doesn't actually save us from the gutter.

Q says, it lifts us up a little?

B says, it saves some people from an actual bad place. The two of us, in our bittersweet middle-class tristesse, it raises us up just high enough to reach the bar in the morning so we can order a double shot of espresso. What we really need.

Q says, if I bought a red Mustang, would you ride in it with me?

B says, no.

Q says, if I bought a red-brick house in the suburbs, would you live there with me?

B says, no.

Q says, if I bought an unforgettable adventure for us like a night at Bakkens Hvile or a weekend in Hanstholm or a night in Las Vegas or tickets to the opera, would you go with me?

B says, no.

Q says, if I bought a stay in a septic tank, would you crawl into it with me and lose yourself with me and lay your whole body down in the reflective liquid and surrender, let yourself float and be reduced to a radical line of thought?

B says, no.

B says, shh, someone is coming.

Q says, who is it?

B raises her arm. The lazy Brazilian wandering spider on the back of her hand has collapsed in exhaustion. Its white membrane has popped, and look! the baby spiders are eagerly scuttling up B's arm, on their way to her neck.

FRIDAY NIGHT: SHH, IT'S the weekend.

Æ is still asleep.

Is it the baby spiders, or is something else tickling B's skin all over?

B knows that someone is coming. Up the stairs, into the living room. Maybe someone's here to help.

Maybe it's a shapely body, a smooth and easygoing body. A cream-in-cake body, the kind that can mediate various neurotic human globs of batter.

A glorious body to collaborate with, to dance with, to spoon with.

Or maybe a harder body, shiny and buff. Out there, showing off the quivering of neurons in their connective tissue.

A glorious body to gesticulate with, to admire.

Or maybe Matthew McConaughey is coming or maybe Michael Fassbender is coming or maybe Ryan Gosling is coming or maybe Benedict Cumberbatch is coming up the stairs.

OMG Matthew McConaughey.

OMG Michael Fassbender.

OMG Benedict Cumberbatch.

OMG Ryan Gosling.

OMG Heath Ledger.

OMG the Hemsworth brothers.

OMG James Franco.

OMG Travis Fimmel.

OMG Rami Malek.

OMG Idris Elba.

OMG Jamie Dornan.

OMG Edward Snowden.

OMG Justin Bieber.

OMG Prince Valiant.

OMG the postman.

OMG, it's Friday.

The heart-shaped bum is sleeping.

And Friday has a pixelated bum.

Sit your arse down!

B and Q on the sofa in front of the TV.

B and Q aren't scared.

We're *not* scared!

The chest freezer in the mudroom: coffin-like sounds.

And then:

Suspense simmers on TV.

Suspense simmers in their bums.

Matthew McConaughey's shadowy demeanour in *True Detective* (2013). Emaciated lover boy, *love bones* and *lovecock*.

It's happening. B and Q's fingers intertwine.

Dive under the blankets.

The television's glinting display in the living room yanks the dark to the front of their awareness: *The Horror Corner.*

Suddenly springing to the back of the sofa.

The spiders rearm themselves. Construct an elastic fort on the ceiling.

The camera follows Matthew McConaughey's character, Rust
Cohle, in the fantastic one-shot scene.
The only fantastic thing in this show
about the relationship between two police officers
Rust and Marty
and their awkward relationships with various women
who either die in extravagant ways
or are passive in sad and trivial ways.
And then there's Rust Cohle's nihilistic prophesies.

The idea that there's no self or free will.
That we're controlled by higher processes.
That life is a trap, a dream, a program.
That we're trapped in a nightmarish loop.
That hypocrisy is the most natural thing.
That delusions are the engine of existence.
Why have children, why live, what does it mean to live, etc. etc.
But somewhere in his nihilism, there's empathy too
in the incessantly masculine, tensed, bombastic
puffing himself up over everything
as if the most extreme form of pessimism still
has an eye for oppression.
Anyway, that sort of saves Rust Cohle.
Rust Cohle can't deal with hypocrisy after all.
You feel it every once in a while in *True Detective*
like in that six-minute one-take night scene
when Rust Cohle goes undercover as an Iron Crusader
and with the other Iron Crusaders
covertly as police
to loot a drug warehouse in *the projects*.
It goes bad, everything is chaos, they end up
shooting at each other anyway.
The rooms are dark, the camera roves around.
We can hear screams between the walls of the houses.
We're taken from house to house
in the dark
and through the backyards
finally over a fence
and Rust Cohle and his hostage Ginger are gone.
But before that:
The expectation of seeing a criminal face illuminated
but then no light
then we've moved on.
Everything flickering.

No sense of how many acts of violence
the camera leaves behind.
Rust Cohle locks a boy in a bathroom, *get in the tub and
stay there.*
We don't know whether the boy will be shot too.
We're not promised justice.
We don't expect any either.
All we get is a masculine desire for justice
which looks good.
Which looks like indignation and passion and lovecock.
And then we're there in its throbbing.
Destruction and indignation's sexy and serious throbbing.
We're in the houses and gardens. In the dark.
Like at a high school party in a nice suburban neighbourhood.
In the dark, maybe some people are making out.
In the dark, maybe someone is dying.

B on the sofa. Hands over the blanket, hands under the blanket.

Rust Cohle, the one everyone wants to fuck, the wet, throbbing nihilism wraps around the thick tree trunks in the
woods where the dead girls sit, magically tied.

B reads about pop nihilism. You don't say *the apocalypse is
coming* anymore, but instead: *the apocalypse is coming, and
I'm not scared.*

B and Q aren't scared!

All four buttocks on the couch: arses don't have free will, but
they aren't scared either!

Rust Cohle eats his own tongue, he's eaten by thousands of
wild girls, torn apart in an old-pink swamp. His lovecock on

his bony body, it squirms in euphoria.

A stalk cock, tied into a thick knot: B admires its enthusiasm.

B and Q are turned on and wet.

Wet hands on the blanket. The old blanket that reeks of kids' pee, the pee on the sofa that no one can see. Tears that no one can see.

Wet eye screens.

Windshield wipers, eyelash hairs.

B and Q, even more turned on, wetter.

Who's the wettest?

And what kind of moisture?

Internal or external?

Discharge or soda?

Tears or crocodile tears?

Filtered crocodile tears, unfiltered crocodile tears?

Filtered apocalypse tears, unfiltered apocalypse tears?

Unhomogenised holy water, homogenised toilet water?

B and Q roll around in cake crumbs on the sofa. The shattered porcelain plates. With four fingers, B firmly grasps her outer lips and stretches them out.

Entry point.

Point of no return.

OMG Santa Claus.

OMG Ronald McDonald.

OMG Baymax.

OMG Jiminy Cricket.

OMG Captain Haddock.

OMG Captain America.

OMG Matthew McConaughey.

OMG Matthew McConaughey is stretched out between two fingers, just like the labia, pulled into slabs of flesh that need to be tenderised now, stretched beyond recognition. In contrast to the slabs of flesh, Matthew McConaughey is a thin string of soft, masculine liquid now, a gleaming tightrope stretched across the living room in the dark.

FRIDAY NIGHT: MAYBE neither B nor Q knows what it means to exist, I mean: to be consummated and polished, I mean: to be real, I mean: to be capable of chilling out; to ask for pleasure and receive pleasure; pleasure as accessible, a minimum goal in life. Maybe neither of them have any idea what they want. To be able to know exactly that, when there isn't time for anything but confusion, or occasionally a full-out argument. An attempt to hold themselves upright, an attempt to create order, an attempt to shave their arms, an attempt to keep the body from blurring, to keep it from re-peatedly deforming and randomly reconstituting itself, or: They have no idea why it never arrives, that perfect moment when they can shut their eyes on the sofa in a state of *completeness* without thinking about aspirin or insurance or the zombie apocalypse or bank robberies or cleaning the oven or myalgia.

B and Q live in the dirt. In a pen. Though they try to come up, and they do try because they're not clear-sighted or resigned enough to admit that maybe they should just stay there: roll-ing around like pigs, muddy, but behind the mud splotches pink and tender, kissing with dirty snouts, crawling on top of each other, if they can actually turn around to feel each other's hides and rub noses through the fence that solidly delineates their square footage, and which makes them con-sider whether they've actually *already* been butchered.

Then he takes her clothes off, he takes his own clothes off, she takes her underwear off. Their clothes are off, they're unemployed and lazy with their clothes off, they haven't showered. They have no clothes on, she has white fluores-cent bum cheeks. She lies down on the sofa. She has unem-ployed squashed-flat buttocks, she doesn't have a thong tan line, she doesn't wear thongs, she has fully-formed big white

bum cheeks. He has small, tanned bum cheeks, he has perfectly controlled bum cheeks. He has hair on his thighs, he
lies down on the sofa, she has black hair on the insides of
her thighs, dark shrubbery on her labia, long black hair she
doesn't trim, which he says smells like pee when he tries to
stick his tongue into it, like through a fence. She planned
it that way: to keep her pubic hair like long strands of seaweed soaked in the piss of a mother of two. Compared to the
blood and the slime after she gave birth, urine seems like a
mild and conciliatory liquid. Compared to being smeared
with blood and slime in the eighth week after giving birth,
the daily squirt of pee in her pubic hair is a kind of perfume,
compared to being a pig in a little pen with twenty other pigs
constantly urinating on each other, she smells fantastic, she
won't groom herself on his terms, his tongue isn't getting
anywhere near her clitoris.

Now, they're very very grown up, great big grownups like
pirates. They're choleric and yelling curses like Captain
Haddock, childish swear words like Onkel Reje. They shout
at each other, into each other's faces. They shout fuck you, go
to hell, useless numbskull, slimy slimeball, interplanetary
goldfish, traitor.

Now B and Q are going out. B is very vain and tries on thousands of dresses before going out. She walks out like a pat-
terned bat, like a yellow buttercup, like a roller girl, into
the world like a parade of women. Q tries on thousands of
hoodies and follows B, dressed in black. He walks alongside
her, a cowl-necked figure, not a parade of cowl-necked figures, just a single one, a pre-washed hero. Who is he exactly.
They walk side by side, maybe holding hands or promenad-
ing at different speeds. Their uncles, aunts, grandmothers,
great-grandmothers, grandfathers, second cousins, fathers

or mothers are dead or about to die. Now B and Q feel infinitely small. They walk faster, into the empty places in the family hierarchy. They're the next in line, they pay the heating bill for the family summer house, they raise their children. They have to reinvent all the rituals, what do you do with the sweets, what do you do with the ugly Christmas decorations, what kinds of people are the kids, what kinds of people are they, and where do people come from when the kids ask. They have an erratic kind of maturity inside them. They grow and then they shake and shrink again. They're so endlessly grown up, time is so elastic, they're so elastic, and their brains are so vast and full of cherries and grapevines and fairy lights and gleaming toilet seats.

2.
A ROOM IN B'S
BRAIN IS ARRANGED
FOR THE DEAD

A ROOM IN B'S BRAIN is arranged for the dead.

Here, the dead are animate.

They arrive, lumbering in heavy wooden clogs, Ecco sandals, slip-ons, pleated skirts, dandelion-printed polyester sundresses, velvet blazers with leather patches sewn onto the elbows with big white stitches, knitwear that looks like it was taken from *Twin Peaks*, blue plaid shirts and grey hospital gowns. They arrive with smiles and energetic bodies. They arrive with punchlines, wiggle their index fingers, gold fillings glittering. They're a mess. They've swapped clothes with each other and with the living. They've just eaten. Their smell, the creeping gasses, are rousing. They behave in unpredictable ways, they are living in an *exaggerated* state.

Their stench: the kind that clings to an animal's pelt.

The animated dead don't have any absence, any grief, inside. They have no awareness of themselves as not-living.

They don't have any regrets.

It's not that they exist in a kind of *nonplace*: a bloodless or acclimatised room, an airport, a waiting room. They aren't in a room with vanilla lattes and club sandwiches, discounted perfumes and lottery tickets.

They aren't in a room with a lavish inventory either, a ballroom, a Baroque garden, an Ikea warehouse. Not a clean room either, somewhere washed and scrubbed and lemony fresh, or that kind of all-white or all-black room, like the ones Jørgen Leth puts his actors in so they appear hyper-human. Their galumphing onstage is already *hyper*.

Maybe they're in a kind of carcass room, a room of half-gnawed tails.

The kind of room where you can't see a whole body part.

Everything is pruned.

And where a rush, like the anticipation in your body before a party, before a masquerade with three lovers and three cast-off fathers and three childhood witches, shoots through your muscles, out of your skin, and becomes a structure.

A kind of path ahead, a nervous and trembling path.

A path you follow, carelessly, with numb toes and wet gravity in your calves, thighs and groin.

3.
DEATH ESSAY

first call

My brother calls and says our father is dead. It's not an un-
imaginable death (our dad: his legs almost didn't work, his
brain was contracting), and it's not the first time I've experienced someone dying. It's a death that brings a sense of relief with it, a death to be expected, but still I know now that
you can't imagine a death, *ever*.

Each time: a new set of heartbeats.

A new set of tumultuous memories.

A frenzied ride on the brain's ghost carousels: his pipe-
smoking friend back in the 80s, a portrait of a sheikh. We
were rolling a ball back and forth, I'm a year and a half, the
ball rolls into a hole in the cardboard box. Typewritten font
on yellowed paper, and the ashtrays are completely full, my
mother empties and washes them. The silk-painted tie with
Christmas elves, I write their nerdy names, Brian, Knud
and Ove, in glitter glue like a runner on the silk, and it's
proudly worn.

The phone immediately loses its innocence. From that day, its
unmotivated ringing will always be associated with nervous-
ness: something happened — who? — where? — an accident.
Something terrible or dramatic. An event you can't shield
yourself from. As if the phone holds an abyss. It holds heavy
speech — it holds distance and delay. It points to the absence
of the body. The absence as an abstraction, and yet: no body,
but an intrusive voice. The voice is the quivering crackle,
which like the worn tip of a pen frays the skin in a frantic
calligraphy, as it sketches its own fleshy figure. On the line,
the figure flutters uneasily: etched flesh, crackling flesh.

Speaking flesh, porous flesh. Not-yet-disintegrated flesh.

The way it crackles in the ear: a taste of the body's future disintegration. Like a *remember you will die* in those Baroque-era paintings: pathos, hourglass and rot. And like the fly-infested grapes and happy-go-lucky skulls in those lush Dutch oil paintings, the phone is a sign of life too. A sign of a *yelping for* life: wanting desperately to live. Wanting to cross the distance to reach life, almost indecently. The phone lures consciousness into the most impractical places: out there where so much of the living is made out of intangible sensations. Out there where I have the urge to fondle the very physics of the intangible.

My brother calls, the trivial death: a telephonic piece of information. I think it makes sense that death arrives with the phone: that the message of a death doesn't pass through the door. That there isn't a criminal assistant standing there with folded hands like an awkward pizza boy. That I find myself out of sync with the concrete physics of death (a holding-hands with the dying, for example) — and in sync with the phone's fleeting, crackling desire for life.

second call

Since I first experienced the death of a family member, death has felt (maybe unreasonably) expansive. Like a fluttering opening to an anterior room. A kind of sensory disorientation that occurs without warning, and which could also be called a state of grief or a prelude to grief or an acknowledgement of having run but never having reached the dead — I haven't been close enough, haven't got it all, there's always more — but which is so full of speed that grief's usual metaphors (something mushy) don't exactly work.

My brain car, oh so fast, it skids through the guardrails; across a field or into a ditch. It slides through thick rhododendron bushes, through withering bamboo hedges, through arabesque intertwined untended plants, buttercups. Through blissful thorn bushes, a hundred years of sleep. Through a wall of dust or sugar, so many sloppy stages. The brain is out of breath. The brain is really restless. And then finally, speeding up, through a dropping barbed-wire fence, into a deserted theme park, full of clichés, we recognise it right away: the brain car squeezes past the carousel's rainbow-coloured grinning horses and hangs out there, spinning around. Little flamboyant clowns sing Patsy Cline's *Crazy*. Coquettish lamps twinkle. The brain car is spat out in a cloud of smoke and rattles on past ruined rides, a Ferris wheel: the brain car takes a ride up on the Ferris wheel, the brain car takes a ride around the Ferris wheel, the brain car keels over, popcorn everywhere, keeps going. Past an abandoned pirate ship with sedated pirates who hang over the bulwarks like worn LEGO figures, like little kids eagerly trapping crabs. The brain car wants to experience more, the brain car will never be full: a lonely chainsaw spinning on the ground. An abandoned playground with brown popsicles in the gravel. Wet fur that looks like seaweed. Pink piggy banks and mannequins with black lace veils taped to their plastic skulls. Big splattering frankfurters arranged to look like swollen fingers, a Santa Claus's hands. Hot dog paper gives the brain car greasy wheels, the brain car ketchup red, totally gross. Small matchboxes and loose hamburger patties with caramelised onions twisted like worms in the gravel, the brain car's motor smokes Western-like, pink candyfloss clouds.

What I'm trying to say is that death is not *only* describable as a physical event. Death is anything but a moment with a beginning and an end. It's not vertical. It's not a fall from the realm of oxygen into the subterranean grave. It's not an ascent from our physical surroundings to somewhere meta-physically divine. Death is more like a territory. It's hori-zontal. A room that can be invaded, expanded and sealed off, something elastic. I can find myself in that space. Be there with my head, be there with my legs. I shoot my arse into that room. Lie down, lean against a wall. Obviously there are two ways to find yourself in the death territory: either you experience death, or you experience someone else dying. Maybe it will be easier to experience my own death than it is to understand death when it seems distant from my own life, when it's devouring the existences around me. But I can't make that demand, I'm not the one dying. My batteries are still half-charged. My bones haven't started to crumble. I am capable and productive. I don't have cancer, I don't have cys-tic fibrosis, I'm too obnoxiously alive, but at the same time I need to understand that death exists. Because every year I have to upgrade my productivity, while I, by watching and getting closer to others, by meeting an old friend and seeing his changed face and his thin hair and wildly bristling eye-brows, understand and accept that I am decaying a little bit every day, am a little more disintegrated on the inside. I play the role of uneasy witness, I'm the neatly dressed stenogra-pher, I take notes on my own demise, I wait around, stand-ing there with my hands in my pockets and biting my nails to shreds, with a cold latte in a paper cup and corny jokes about time passing behind my ear.

I have a marbled photo album from 1993 under my arm. It contains a picture of my father wearing a red clown nose. In another picture, he's holding my hair up with three hands: two real, one rubber hand. That rubber hand is my thirteenth birthday present. The surface of the hand is clammy, the colour more animal than human. Death is a memory and a material and a shudder. The hand awakens my tenderness. I can't let it go. I carry it around in moving boxes, a totem, a prosthesis. A clammy assistant to my secluded computer life, a prop for the writing process: the hand's sallow dead-life surface tells me something about the conflicting state of power and powerlessness I step into every time I try to formulate an opinion about something, every time I start moving into a style. The hand's fingertips have been inside nostrils and pantylines and become part of my brain's exercises in thinking through transition and decay. Now it lives in my daughter's drawer. She plays curiously and carelessly with it, she bangs it on her little brother's head. I shudder when she puts it on my thigh.

Bottle openers and sweet cherries, sucked cherry pits, mussel shells, painted eggs. Horseshoes, cigar boxes, chess pieces, crumbled chocolate, nose trimmers. All the nostalgic objects jammed into a rucksack, velcroed shut, then I tell my boyfriend that I'm going into the city to drink a lonely cortado at a café and work in peace, while I flap into the elastic death territory, which could also be described as the process by which the experience of death matures inside me — a tough string of memories, acknowledgements and inner dialogues — it gushes through my consciousness without a chronology, without any regard for systems, without any regard for objectivity, without any regard for neatness, without any regard for moderation, without any regard for climaxes or narrative desire, without any regard for chapter titles, paragraphs or indents, without any regard for confectionery, cake or cocktail parties, without any regard for reconciliation, without any regard for anger, except the anger constantly lurking like background music.

Without any respect for the dead.

Nevertheless, as if the dead were throwing a party (this is how much faith we have in the dead and in death: he/her/they will always be throwing a party, there's always something to celebrate!): a party decorated with the corniest jokes, piles of images and bird shit. Decorated with line-dancing memories. Or: memories that dance a medieval death dance, skeletons and pudgy barons holding hands. Or a contemporary dance of the dead: immigrants waiting for their green cards, and members of all the Danish political parties holding hands. And floating around: half-phrases, jokes and intonations that don't add up to a logical portrait of the dead, but rather encrypt each other, make each other more difficult to understand, so the portrait starts to teeter.

The gnawed versus the bloody sublime.

We've seen it before, the cadaver and the maggots, but it's always a little fascinating. Just try YouTube, for example: *Time lapse of a dead pig decaying.*

And I report back into the living like this. Which is to say, either I'm speaking or I'm writing. Or at least I want to. While I'm being lazy, waiting for the right form to arrive, I take a walk and make a few unaccustomed movements with my arms, twist my hips, shake my head. Maybe I have a blue pen that stains. Maybe a laptop, a keyboard full of crumbs and hair. Maybe a piece of chalk so I can draw instructions on the asphalt. The outline of a body: it's too banal. Four points bound by a line, a cloud, a gun. I am already tired of my ideas, and anxious, but also don't care: because the death territory with all its transience and elasticity doesn't have an up or a down, but rather contains a bankrupt transcendence, a punctured divinity, a limitless rumbling, a witty noirish nothingness, a hymnal din; then I can stay here without reporting back to any solemn authority. It's a relief. Everything becomes simpler. Or becomes more varied and suspenseful, but also more accessible, as if I can just nudge something a bit and it will yield. I'm on the floor. Maybe I'm lying down. Maybe I'm sitting up. Maybe I suddenly stand up straight and take a few little hops in place, a kind of dance move. My shoes are shiny and hysterical, there are bows on their tips, they're perfectly set with their stiff slightly faded yellowish look, the black glossiness that surrounds them. Maybe the weight of my body is pulling me in my jump down to the floor, towards the underworld, I'm heavy and corporeal, and my physique is impressive (like Gene Kelly); maybe the jump sends my heavy body effortlessly upwards in a weightless state, I'm elegant and flexible, a seductive insect (like Fred Astaire). Maybe I take a look around: a fishing boat, a diesel engine, an old rap song from 1998, a Christmas carol about *elk, mammals, the apple of my eye, a reindeer.* Maybe I'm daydreaming about an old flame, *gonna lay down*, lazily on the floor. I press two wet fingers against my clitoris, move them around in a semicircle, almost without touching; and the death territory is now an elastic teenage space of horny fantasies, a mirror between my legs, a desirable mood, we long for that room where so much is happening all the time, so many unfinished thoughts are hatched, so many conflicting psychologies, what's the point anyway, what's driving everyone else, what are we supposed to be doing, the flakes of splintered mirror are glued together on the ceiling in a meticulously chosen zigzag pattern, the wall is burgundy red, Tori Amos is singing in "Icicle" about the girl masturbating in her room, isolated from the rest of her family and their evening prayer and ideas about what flesh is *and when my hand touches myself, I can finally rest my head, and when they say take of his body, I think I'll take from mine instead*, but it's not because I want to privilege masturbation as a tool of liberation or redemption from whatever, from grief or melancholy, or as a tool of insight or as a tool of revolt, that would give it way too much power. Still, masturbation is a kind of investigative movement that reaches past the individual body: even in the most intimate, banal sexual fantasies that follow the tics of masturbation, you are never alone. The choreography of desire is full of tentacles, dreamy images of a being-together. I'm still in here, maybe I'll have some company. Maybe from the little circus performer who is twisting in the corner, attention-seeking. Maybe from two wrinkled, flower-clad ladies drinking coffee and singing *Singin' in the Rain*. Maybe from the little figure over there, you can't feel it's rotten until you've stuck your hands down into it and really kneaded, soft bones and sharp bones.

third call

The idea of failed transcendence has to do with my curiosity about the word *cryptos*, the word for burial chamber, which the English author Tom McCarthy writes about. In Greek, it means hidden, but also contains the meaning of *encrypt*. To encode, to receive codes, to decode codes.

In Jean Cocteau's surrealist retelling of the Orpheus myth *Orphée*, from 1950, the crypt is a soundscape.

In the film, the dead poet Cégeste transmits signals from the underworld through the car radio.

Orphée listens. He's the hero of the film. Orphée is played

by the gorgeous Jean Marais, who is like a carved sculpture. He's a cowboy in marble. His cheeks are rough but would quickly start to shine if everyone rubbed their hands over him in arousal. I know that everyone would choose exactly the cheeks, not the arse or the dick.

Orphée becomes obsessed with sitting in the car in the garage when no one is watching, and listening to the abstract, poetic messages from his friend, the dead poet Cégeste, whose voice fills the car. The messages sound like: *Listen, the bird paints with its fingers, twice. I repeat...* and then it repeats. Or: *Silence moves faster when it is played in reverse. Listen, twice.* And someone is counting, and there's static and crackling.

Orphée's obsession with these codes makes me think of World War II, when the British Secret Service transmitted similar codes into an occupied France, hundreds of poetic verses. Only one out of every two hundred meant something in the game of war and might be decoded if you searched long enough for repetitions. Orphée is crazy about codes. Orphée doesn't want meaning but mysteries. Death is hidden, and now it's calling to Orphée in signs. Death, a slow speaker voice. Crackle, crunch. The small interior of the car becomes a whole world, a soundscape. A poetic territory, where the voice of the dead friend floats through the air, and death is brought to life. Orphée is turned on. Orphée is full of technological longing. Radio technology — a technology that, in an exemplary way, contains the idea of absence, transmitting something across a distance, transmitting something that's already happened — gives Orphée an image of death. It's captivating, and Orphée is listening.

I imagine a world made of signs: of unofficial, imperceptible forms of language. But what does that mean for my own attempt to understand death? What does it mean that the death territory is sending disorienting signals to Orphée? That death is a crackle and a crunch, a ride in the brain's car? Is death always followed by the technological? Is death always encrypted? Is it a code to be broken? Does it lie in wait like an erotic secret? A current of meaning underneath everything else? Is death's language unofficial and imperceptible, and does death thereby assume a subversive character? Is the language of love in *Orphée* just as unofficial? Does it matter that Jean Cocteau was Jean Marais's lover — that an everyday, a real love is happening outside the sensory space of the screen — that love in a way is encrypted to the film's audience? That love that isn't heterosexual is encrypted? That even the film's love might be encrypted: that it's mysterious, like in the scene where Orphée's girlfriend Eurydice is in the back seat of the car, and Orphée makes eye contact with her in the mirror so that she vanishes — *poof*, a film trick — maybe back to the death territory forever? Is love always impossible to account for, is love an underworld, like death? Is encryption a necessary condition for eroticism and devotion? Or a necessary condition for vanishing? Does life really have the power? Does life puff itself up, while love and death's rebel soldiers are napping and lying in wait to overthrow it all?

If I listen to my father's CDs from beginning to end, if I listen to the entire Billie Holiday boxset *God Bless the Child* or *Ode to my Family* with the Cranberries (the only one of my silly pop songs he fell in love with, he listened to it over and over in his room), if I listen to them on repeat and backwards, like the American parents in the 1990s who were searching for Satanic messages on their kids' Motörhead albums — will I decode the music, will a new language emerge — will there be a message from my dad in the silly beats and growling voices, a rumble from the death territory — will I get a new soundscape for my memories?

<u>fourth call</u>

My boyfriend and I open the door to the catacombs in Rome. The crypt is located many, many steps down the stairs. We can hear the soles of our shoes on the steps. Then we're in the *Wunderkammer*. Here, the wall has been built as an enormous shelving system, not for books but for bones. The legs are neatly and symmetrically arranged on small shelves. I take my boyfriend's hand and feel his knuckles, the edges in his fingers. He pretends to crack an egg on my knee, I'm about to fall. On the inside we must be more entangled than that, less neat. The princes are lying here, mummified and glittering. In the next crypt are lamps made from human bones. The cosiness is wonderfully morbid. It's so bizarre that death is glittering for a private audience even though people are being killed everywhere: that wretched form of death is hidden away. I imagine our living room, in the November darkness, morbid too, the scene set with television, sofa, speakers, carved pumpkins and other objects that one or more bodies, animals and organisms, have died to create, but that we're attached to because they, by virtue of their furry, shiny, inciting structures, make nature's peculiarity appear clearer and less threatening. In the Himalayas, there's not enough wood to burn the bodies of the dead. The undertaker accompanies the family to the vulture's preferred location, after the family says their goodbyes he dismembers every last bit of the deceased. He tosses the body parts into the sky. The vultures strike and eat right away. The crypt is in the air, and it's full of dramatic, beautiful beaks.

Maybe the crypt is old-fashioned and boring. I mean — the idea of death as something hidden doesn't actually interest me at all. I don't care to think in riddles, to wait for illuminated words from the dead, from my father, from my grandmother, from my two aunts, from Olof Palme, from Madame Blavatsky, from Chantal Akerman, from Inger Christensen, from Nefertiti. Maybe death is esoteric — introverted and hidden — to the extent that the esoteric holds an attempt to reenchant a world which, in its external forms, has stalled out, has become stiff and cold and predictable — but death isn't distant even though it communicates from a place that isn't the everyday, that can't be grasped or articulated. Death is not an undercurrent of meaning, unofficial and intangible.

Death is not an undercurrent of meaning when the dead are lying on display, nicely made up with dark red cheeks and big, snail-like eyebrows. When you can see the dead and hold the dead's hand and say a tactile goodbye. Death is not an undercurrent of meaning when the dead's faces are blown up in press photos, photocopies, posters, everywhere in the city and everywhere online in a globally narrated visual funeral parade. Death is not an undercurrent of meaning when we know exactly how cancer cells multiply in a lung and outnumber the healthy cells and tissue structures and damage the oxygen supply. Death is not an undercurrent of meaning when the brain of the deceased is pulled out through the nose on a hook, when the belly is gently sliced open so the guts, muscles and blood can be dug out of the body's casing. When the hollowed body is subsequently filled with liquid plastic and sewn back up, now a preserved container that can exist for months as a statuesque mummy in the dim light of the bedroom, which can be worshipped like an eminent figure, someone who will never darken because the dark and shrunken body would be perceived as macabre — as if the body in its living life also represented something entirely specific and went through life that way, statuesque and majestic and white — before it, in a coffin, is lowered into the ground and has a difficult time decomposing, the body doesn't want to rot, it's too decorated and hygienic to bear decay's horror, why isn't there any food for the worms? Death is not an undercurrent of meaning when the powers of imagination aren't encrypted. When there is contact in the brain. When the brain says what others are thinking. I touch my father's corpse, especially the hands. They're cold. There are bits of food in his beard, I don't know whether anyone else has noticed. Maybe bits of egg, something bright and insignificant, small dots melted into the grey of his beard. It makes him a sadder figure — like a child who hasn't been properly taken care of — but also more alive: he ate eggs every day for lunch, I wonder whether he was still served eggs in the nursing home where he spent the last two months of his life, I think about the egg as a crucial constant in his life, I search for proof that it wasn't a lack of eggs that took away the last of his strength. When I look at the corpse, I try to identify with it — here is a body like mine. I call the hands ice cold, but even the words *ice cold* — just like the word *heavy* or the word *pink* or the word *loving* — is an attempt to humanise the foreign body. In that sense, there's no language I can accept as precise enough for the experience of death. That's my index finger on the surface of his skin. The finger pad against the hand's lifeless peach fuzz. The idea of identification through shared DNA. I'm not sure what I should do with language. Still, I try to test language out. I try to tell my girlfriends about death. I tell my boyfriend about death. I tell my daughter about death. I tell a stranger on a plane about death. I write a smug poem about death. I make a performance about death. I stage a musical about death. I paint an acrylic painting about death. I recite a sonnet about death. And then I try again. What I write turns into small spots on the surface of the physical yet abstract space of death, or I let fantasies about the death space rub off on what I'm writing. Can a text be stripped of the usual human codes? Can a text be an organism without consciousness, a mucus thread between blades of grass? I'm not talking about immaterial text, about text that's been reprogrammed into a form capable of existing in a distant galaxy. I don't want to think of what I'm writing as unreadable or invisible. I'm actually just wondering if a text can be a corpse? Can a text represent death's incomprehensibility, does the text ever really represent anything anyway?

The person I'm in love with often says the same sweet words, but with a twist. Then it's followed by something surprising. A new sentence trails behind like a strange tail. I thought that I could respond, that I could just respond as usual, but now I don't have an answer. Or maybe suddenly, I have so many, but none of them have any form yet, and inside me something starts to break, he's given me something. A discomfort, now I'm looking inside myself, and I look at him. I want to keep going, but what, I don't know with what. I end up here: Language comes to life for me when words change meaning, when the same words are constantly experienced as new, when the experience of the foreignness of these words makes new words take shape inside me. An answer is coming. Death comes to life for me when it's monumentally unique and at the same time is not. When it's always being repeated, always in process as a constant reinterpretation of itself, we don't just say, then he died, so we'll never have to experience death again, on the contrary, now we'll have to experience it again and again, *we ain't seen nothing yet*, there are the *really old ones*, I talk to them over coffee, the

Methuselahs, collapsed backs, coarse hairs on their chins, snake eyes, tears, I observe their routines, I scan them for grief, how are they getting through this, I think, sneaking a sentence in here and there, he's dead too, she's dead too, now she's dead, he died years ago you know, they're all dead now, that was back when x was alive, but of course x isn't here anymore, nor y, z or q either, nor 867 and 534 and 3,086 for that matter, they're all dead, all of life's agents have kicked the bucket, now they exist in an internal drama, maybe in a never-finished conversation, maintained by a matter-of-fact grief, like guests at a sweet little brain cabaret, it never stops, it'll never stop, from now on it'll just keep going on, come on then, just die, get going, will you.

Death is actually like a glowing match for the text, the writing process a glowing match for the warm finger on the ice-cold hand, the dead beard on the living egg.

The ice-cold hand is difficult to ignore. The ice-coldness in the skin. I can't sleep when it's too cold. I don't want to have sex, I get goosebumps everywhere. Love is an undercurrent of meaning, but love is also direct. The person I'm in love with says things I never thought anyone would say to me. Which he never thought he would say to anyone. Both of us might have experienced these words before, but can't remember them anymore. Maybe we've been sleeping in the meanwhile. We can't remember me sitting on his dick while the window was open. I don't think I can respond. But I've already opened my mouth, my tongue is sticking out. Is it always out. Belly skin, bum cheeks, still like ice under the duvet in the winter night, legs slowly warming up, thighs softer, almost boiling, speckled red like flushed cheeks, labia full of blood, now flapping on either side, it's all open, the hairs curl an extra loop, the adrenaline makes my belly flatten, my back curve, my thighs can suddenly open wide, each body part has its own life. The limbs fall slowly from the torso, the body parts are separated. In Matthew Barney's film *Drawing Restraint 9,* the two lovers, passengers on a Japanese whaler, take turns cutting long strips of flesh from each other's legs in a slow, ritualistic scene. They eat the strips, roll them into sushi-like bites; now they've devoured almost everything. They slice the last hunk off the thighs, reluctantly embrace, dive into the water, the sliced-off leg-stumps turn into waving whale tails, and the lovers finally turn into whales themselves. He's inside me, he's sitting up, my foot on his shoulder, he bites my toe. My big toenail cuts his gums, blood comes out, we're surprised, the little splash of blood outdoes almost all the blood that streamed out of me yesterday, it was the end of my period, but that blood was still expected. It was cyclical. This blood has its very own parodic unease. In a writing workshop I have the students write a letter to a body part they might have neglected, that bothers them; a tender address. Afterwards, they work in groups to join their texts into a single monster body, they read their monster texts aloud, a back on top of a head, lips on top of toes. Occasionally an orgasm feels specific, its dramaturgy is local, it dilates on the right side of the body or runs through the left foot. It's hard to know if it's already over; was it just a little comfy this time? Suddenly my consciousness didn't just shut off, that feeling of bewilderment never turned up. Suddenly, I had the feeling of observing my own euphoria at a distance. Looking at my body and his body in their positions, right there, posed in arousal, looking at them like new strange limbs, like objects. It feels disappointing, but also teasing, disappointment eye-opening in all its practicality. We hold our poses only until we fall apart again, a little like old Barbie dolls. I look down into the pot: the grey-white foam spots on the boiled broccoli that we serve to the kids with meat sauce. I keep fishing up the foam with a spatula, it's so ugly, but so eager to exist.

I don't want to deal with the crypt anymore, but what about my father's body? He's only just died, I still have time to bury him!

I make a series of attempts.

I bury his body in a crypt, but not the kind where I'll have to wave down into some sublime depths to come to terms with my grief. I try to imagine the crypt as something else:

I try to think of the crypt as both fleshy and fluffy.

I try to think of a place where death is directly experienced, but still not understood as something complete. Where death and its literal expression — the corpse — is sensed as parts of a narrative that is constantly expanding. Death also holds all the life that we didn't get to have. Or: Death is a cue that strengthens your conceptions of life, the already lived and the life that's coming. In that sense, I can't avoid the feeling of *something more*, the feeling I get when I talk to an old friend, my mother, my boyfriend: that we said the most banal and honest things we could in that moment, but that there are so many other versions of us and of the things we say. There is always more. In the same way, death is not a darkness, but what makes me imagine endless variations of my father's life, of all other kinds of life and of the death that is already inside us.

First I bury the corpse in the body's crypt. I'm never alone in my body, and I think that there must be room for others. Come on in, Dad, *squeeze*. Inside, a billion bacteria are frolicking about: my beloved collaborators. They hold me up, stabilise my mood. They're active, a happy micro-society inside me, invisible to my consciousness. I will never understand their relationships to each other, their emotional lives, if those exist inside them. Their tears and romances operate on another scale. Maybe they have orgies, maybe they swap partners at a rate I would never be able to imagine, and when bacteria die, what do they do then, do they all decay at the same rate? At first I don't know how I'll get my father's corpse lowered into me: a meal, an operation? When he's finally arrived in my intestines, I don't get to say a proper goodbye, or I can't see him, and I almost regret it. I lie awake all night, listening to my belly growling. Has my father already become a family of bacteria? Has he had new kids in my duodenum? A new girlfriend? Does he love them more than he loved me and my brother and my mother? Are families more beautiful in the intestinal world, less destructive? I wake up and need to speak. I sing "I'll Be Seeing You" really loudly in the bathroom. I record my own voice on my phone. My song plays on repeat in bed close to my ear, I fall asleep.

Then I bury the corpse again. I bury it in pockets of air, in a cloud. I simply throw the body upwards, and I sense it being caught. I imagine a crypt that exists in the atmosphere. A buzzing crypt that exists where all the data is stored. Maybe there's room for the dead here. Now my hands are empty. I buy a pastry with black icing. At night I gobble it down and watch *Citizenfour*, the documentary about Ed Snowden. I fall immediately for Snowden's idealistic eloquence, he tells us all about the profit-related motives of surveillance. Now I've buried the corpse in a surveillance crypt. The corpse is seen without itself knowing what or whom it sees. The crypt doesn't hide the body: it effortlessly floats away. Instead the crypt stands for all of the ubiquitous mechanisms imperceptibly controlling us, those which never stop registering our actions, but which never let themselves be recognised. But it doesn't really matter anymore: the corpse can't surf the web anymore, throw likes at a cute baby picture or archive all its transactions. The corpse can't move, surveilled, through town anymore, stand on a street corner under a CCTV camera. The corpse is home free, it doesn't care about its private life or its integrity. In that sense, the corpse is shameless, but also seriously dead: the corpse doesn't change like I change, slowly slipping into an increasingly paranoid and exhibitionist state, exaggeratedly aware of everything and everyone, suspicious and analysing, oversharing, speed-talking, sugar-eating (who's watching me eat cake?! Who's watching me eat cake AGAIN!? PLEASE does anyone want to watch me eat cake!?!). Maybe an ideal state in which to meet the world right now, a friend says to me: we end up resembling the structures that surround us.

But I don't believe that at this moment. Everything is both inside me and outside me. I can't control anything at all. But I don't want to submit either. I don't want to give in to a structure, I would rather believe I can slide through it.

That's why I finally bury the body in three different choreographies.

Movement might overcome the feeling of stagnation and that's why I want to put some movement into the system.

The corpse gets to move too!

Out on the floor everybody!!

The first dance is a classic quickstep. Come on, Dad, we can do it, you can stand on my feet, slow-quick-quick-slow.

The second dance takes place in the laboratory. We visit my older brother at his workplace. My father's body and I move carefully through the white laboratories of the State Serum Institute. We're ready to open ourselves to the experiments, we're ready to taste some of those listeria sausages, we're not afraid of listeria. We grab some tweezers, lick the edges of petri dishes, open freezer doors, sniff cellular structures. I hold my father's corpse's head. He looks into the microscope through his closed eye, there's an impression like a coin on his eyelid. We hang out here for a little while and dance, among fingers, tools, ingredients.

The last dance unfolds in Maya Deren's *Ritual in Transfigured Time* (watch it on YouTube). I make my father's corpse dance along in the silent black-and-white film from 1946. As soon as we've arrived, I recognise the film. I know it starts with two women, Maya Deren, the white Russian-Jewish immigrant, and Rita Christiani, the black immigrant from Trinidad, fleeing a claustrophobic party in a living room full of white people. A cut, a new scene: Rita Christiani, a line of dancing women and a tall, athletic man are now moving through a park. The man spins the women around in an exaggerated twirl. Then their bodies freeze. The man freezes too, he turns into a sculpture on a pedestal. Then he moves again, like a robot. And here we are, my father's corpse and me, in the park. We aren't dancing, but sitting on the grass. I support my father's body, holding him up so he can watch. The tall man is chasing Rita Christiani with aggressive, ecstatic leaps. She drifts further and further out in a sea that is only getting deeper. Then suddenly she turns into Maya Deren in an elegant doubling. My father's corpse and I are still sitting, looking out over the sea after them. We're still in

the movie. Then the park is gone, the sea is gone, and suddenly we're being spun around. The image is in negative,
now we're in negative. We're altogether white and cottony
against a black background. We float through the movie's
last thirty seconds with Rita Christiani, whose lace veil is
rustling around her: we can't tell whether she's rising or
falling, whether she's an angel or a white corpse against a
black background, a bride or a mourner. I want to melt together with the two women. It's as if they've escaped from
a violent fantasy, from the manic, aggressive suitor who's
been chasing them across the landscape, but also from the
racism lurking in the social space because it's mainly the
black woman, Rita Christiani, who's being followed. Now
they've both ended up here, maybe fused together as a kind
of defence, with me and my father's corpse as eager guests:
outside the social, in a death dance, floating through a beautiful white atom-bomb cloud. I'm not worried for the wom-
en. After having seen them dance I have the feeling they're
working together, that their dancing movements make
change possible. Each turn is so graceful, each leap so ec-
centric. So surprising. As I drift away into a world where everything is wrong side out, I think that maybe choreography
is a structure that splits up bodies — dissects them into gestures, isolated movements, body parts — to put them back
together again as new imaginary worlds, structures and relationships with other bodies. My father's corpse and I keep
floating, the film isn't over yet: My father's corpse doesn't
have a veil, but his beard is like lace. It parts and unfurls
in long strands. I should be worried for him. I know that my
father's corpse has a questionable status for the woman in
here. Not only because he's a man. Not only because he's a
white man. He's also dead. In death there's still a body, still
a gender, still a story. And in death there can be a kind of
power: what's been finished can make you feel something

monumental. Like the story about all the dead pop stars in 2016. Nuances disappear, criminals become heroes. But I end up deciding with my father's corpse that we won't give up: that we're on the women's side, and that we'll show them our love, our flexibility, our dedication to the common good. I shout to Rita Christiani's floating body that if my father had been young today, he'd be going to the movies with his girlfriend to see all Maya Deren's movies, eating popcorn and holding hands. He would have loved her sensual and chaotic images. I have a gentle hold on the long strands of my father's corpse's beard, as if I were holding him on a leash. My father's body is stiff, and his limbs don't fall off so easily, don't slide so easily back on, but he's still enjoying this, I can tell. We fly around the black room inside our white backwards-facing bodies, moving at terrible speed.

fifth call

After the burials I can no longer find my father's body. It makes me nervous. I don't know where he's ended up. I'm afraid of what my mother will say. I think about my mother. I call out to him — I call very carefully.

I think about the word *choreography*, which has roots in the ancient Greek word *khoreia*. The word describes both the dance itself and the circular enclosure where the dance takes place. Choreography is thereby closely connected to *the choir* — and with the worlds, structures and patterns narrated by the choir that emerge from it and are experienced within it. Maybe choreography and choir can also contain the violent and uncomfortable. Maybe violence's power can be tamed here.

But I can't be a choir on my own: I suddenly and acutely miss my mother and the rest of my family, I miss all my ex-boy-friends and all my old friends, all the strangers on the plane and the charter trip and at the club, I miss my kids and all my unborn kids and all the idiots on TV and all the serving staff in all the cafés.

A few years later, I go to the movies to see Jeppe Rønde's *Bridgend*. The plot reminds me of *The Children*, where a group of kids are possessed by spirits and murder their parents. But *Bridgend* isn't a story of parenthood. Besides, I've never been interested in killing my family. But I am interested in the relationship between death and family and the passages between them: in grief and memory, in broken connections and in summoning what's been lost. In the loneliness and the community that exist in our conceptions of what a life is, and what a death is.

Bridgend takes place in a small Welsh town. A group of ill-adjusted teens start their own cult of the dead. They take turns committing suicide — hang themselves, throw them-selves in front of trains — and each time another friend dies, they charge into the woods to drink themselves stupid and skinny dip euphorically in the icy water and party hard and disillusioned, and chant the name of the deceased in a screaming choir: MARK, MARK, MARK!! In *Bridgend*, the youth rebel against the parents who treat them badly, busy with their own problems. The parents that always let you down. But instead of killing the overlords — the parents — the teenagers kill themselves. They take ownership. They create a temporary free space where guilt can't be assigned: The teenagers don't even see each other's bodies, the police are the ones cutting the dead bodies down from the trees. Their rebellion is tragic because it's masochistic — but so is parenthood. The difference is that the teenagers in *Bridgend* create a space where they can summon one of their own. When you kill the father, his power only grows — his absence amplifies his adoration. When Louise Bourgeois visualises patricide in her sculpture *The Destruction of the Father* — a dreamy scenario in red-illuminated plaster and bubbling, swollen latex: a dinner table/bed with a skin-like surface onto which the kids can pull the man of the house and tear him apart — the father is at the centre of the artist's obsessive re-living of the pain he once inflicted on his children: Daddy returns again and again and again as fodder in the children's bodies and in Bourgeois's brain.

But in *Bridgend* the father is entirely undermined — here, it's the teenagers' power that is steadily growing, cultic, out of proportion. I don't know if that's how you call on the dead: MARK, MARK, MARK!

The call, as in the call and response, the response is already there before the call goes out. You're already in something.

Before I even begin to call, I can feel that a response is coming. The response tightens my skin. So I call the person I'm in love with. Call everyone I've been in love with. But I'm already surrounded by him. He's already there. They're all already there. Ready to respond. Surrounded by me. By my response. I'm already there. He already has a question. They've all had their questions. Been in love like me. There's already a space. It's been shaped by our expectations, our ignorance. The world's fundamental unease turned into suspense. Which makes us open. Temporarily. There's already a kind of feedback loop between us. In the space. Nothing else is supposed to happen. Nothing else can happen. We need to be in this space and then leave it. Not be in it. Not let ourselves be swallowed. Go now. It'll hurt if we stay. It hurts now. Go on your way. I didn't know if I could kiss you, he says. We didn't know if we could kiss you, they all say. You didn't know? I ask. We don't know when something starts. How much pain it can cause. We've forgotten our anxiety, our cockiness. Fuck all of you. You had already put your hand on my lower back, the second before you asked if you should kiss me, before you knew what I would say. Before it was even something that could happen. Fuck you. My answer moved your hand around, it landed sweaty on my body, then I started to hear all of the sounds that came from you.

I'm twenty-six, I'm sleeping with the book *Angry Women* under my pillow. I read an interview with the singer Diamanda Galás again and again. On repeat. Like with a song. I listen to the CD called *Plague Mass*. It's almost unbearable to listen to. *Listen to this CD in a completely dark room on max volume.* I do. In a performance of *Plague Mass*, Diamanda Galás sings her growling, whispering sentences inside a church after she is lowered from the vaults covered in blood in a black BDSM outfit. Galás sings about the AIDS crisis in the 1980s: about how the Catholic church was passive and condemned the many people infected in the homosexual community, considered their lives sinful and depraved and refused to teach or discuss HIV or AIDS. Galás lost her brother to the disease. The song's voodoo-like power isn't random. Galás stages a death territory. A space that is about grief, about revenge. To remember those who died, shamed and maybe isolated from their families or loved ones. Galás sings in a hymnal, gurgling, screeching way; occasionally she hisses incredibly loud. Electronic sounds cut in. And suddenly a cascade of words. Speaking in tongues, the language of the church shaken up. It's the most physical sound I know, it's both terrifying and ridiculously fun. I can't describe it better, but I also can't stop listening: Galás conjures

an intimate architecture of sound that gives me the chance
to take part in a collective grief even though I'm far away
from the events she's singing about. I'm touched. The sound
can touch me. I collapse in laughter. Completely surrounded
by the music's ridiculous restlessness shouting: We are des-
perate! Justice is pulverised! Let's try again with all we've
got! I can't look away from the pain there, even though it
isn't mine. I feel like someone arming themselves: making
preparations to grieve someday. I wish that all deaths were
given a voice like Galás's. I don't think there are any limits
or rules for when you can call on someone, or be called on. I
don't think you can ever know what you're setting in motion
when you start to call.

Every day, there's someone calling. Not only from the speaker. Not only on the street. But also unexpected interpola-
tions: from the teddy bear's eye. From the bottom of a jar of
mustard or out of a Disney movie. Up from my nailbeds.

In a way, I'm also constantly shouting at myself with my
tongue folded in a wonderful knot to lead the sound back
into my skull with a big whoosh, every day some kind of power arrests me from the inside or the outside YOU BIG POOPY
DOGHEAD, SALLOW SOUPY BODY, PUDDING BELLY BUTTON,
SLOPPY MUM BODY, HOARDER, FATTY, PASSIVE MEATPOTATO,
HYPOCRITE, SENTIMENTAL FOOL, I turn into a grainy face on
a Skype call with my boyfriend or my daughter or my friend
or my mother, I'm rainbow-coloured on the screen, coagulat-
ed in someone else's living room, I'm still being called, I get
nervous, I think about the movie *Unfriended* where a hacker
ghost kills a bunch of teenagers on Skype, hey how's it going,
I can't see you, you bitch, oh, wait, you're frozen, what time is
it over there, hi, my daughter, how are you, hey sweetie, there
you are, now I can see you, now I can hear you, now your face

is gone again.

Everything that crunches and mumbles interpolates too. And everything that doesn't make a sound. I'm not thinking about calling as literal. Something sizzling on a frying pan. The internet saying *surf me.*

The thought of the call quickly becomes a longing to be touched: The sound is material. *Plague Mass* is over. I rub my face. I grasp my earlobes firmly. I listen to nostalgic music. An earworm makes it into my head. The almost not-singing voices on Tricky's 1993 album *Maxinquaye* penetrates my body, invades my brain's territory in a drowsy, sexy, half-eaten agitation. I was far too young to understand the words the first time I heard the songs, far too young to feel anything but a craving to be closer to the world. I wasn't having any visible existential crisis, it was prestigious to be totally fucked, I couldn't perform that feeling, I felt excluded from it. *I drink till I'm drunk, and I smoke till I'm senseless*, Martina sings, I'm fourteen and a virgin and secretly smoking those pink cigarettes with golden filters, not knowing how to inhale. But I still loved Tricky's aggressive intimacy. I think about being fondled. About a fleshy invocation. Intimate and harassing. About everyone who's put a hand on my arse, an arm around my waist when I didn't want it. About the uncertain intermediary of every touch. I catch myself caring for men with melancholic, eager Bambi eyes who grope other people, take every occasion to *touch*, the awkwardness of it. Because I want to be desired. Because it's nice when men make the rounds that way, don't demand any exalted worship, don't need to talk for what seems like an eternity, just expose their horniness, make themselves available to women's need for approval and play, for women's desire. I'd like men to be that way: available, submissive.

So that he can indulge himself a little, since after all he's the one keeping the patriarchy cooking. But just as quickly I experience that way-too-simple, reckless form of touch as uncomfortable. An arm around the waist, it's squeezing, what am I supposed to do, I don't want it, I can't get out now, I want to get out now, an arm around my shoulders, it's squeezing and squeezing, my mouth almost squashed against his nipple, I could almost suck on it.

I've written about crypts: the crypts of the body, of air, of movement. I should write about the crypt of the grope.

I am twenty-seven, at that point I don't understand how my boyfriend can feel groped by a literary text. I learn the abstract meaning of the word grope. The text is uncannily similar to one of his own, but it's been written by a younger guy and attached to his application to the Danish Academy of Creative Writing. The text doesn't intend to grope, but is a victim of reading's contagious power. It eagerly intrudes. I think my boyfriend finds it shameless and overeager. At any second it could be revealed as an imposter, it just really wants to be part of something. But even when it's found out, it's still part of something. Actually, it's full of love. Eventually no one cares about who copied whom. The two texts have touched each other, and it isn't important who came first.

Maybe it's like this?:

Groping is physical and local. It's first felt in the body. The call is different, it's first felt in the nervous system; it's diffuse, suddenly it's everywhere.

I walk around with hands hanging out of my underwear. Where did they come from, how am I controlling them? I have all of these hands hanging there like a vine, and I can dangle them around, I can wear them like jewellery, I joke around with them if I don't break down first, sixteen rubber hands coming out of my underwear, seventeen, every day they give me hundreds of small loose rubbery overconfident orgasms.

sixth call

And the phone's call, the phone's fondle?

I circle the ringing phone. I don't pick up, pick up right before the call is broken off. I pick up the receiver with a kind of energetic defiance. The phone triggers a nervous reaction inside me. I can't accept that someone wants something from me in such a possessive way. Do you wanna play?... We're missing a payment from... I have to ask you something... Isn't it fantastic what we're doing for the refugees here at Amnesty... What's going on, cracks in your voice... frog in the throat... you sound fragile, are you okay? Are you a fully-formed persona, are you a limp and incoherent one? Does your voice draw with an old pencil, does it spray from a fat can?

The ring tone is monstrous, the sound is soon gone. I only have a margin of seconds before I have to speak and receive speech, open my ear, let myself occupy and be occupied, be ready for that kind of submission — a potential humiliation — to have the words pulled out of me, but not have the gestures to deflect and seduce and insist.

Eyes can close, and the mouth.

But not the ears.

As if the body needs a receptor that the self can't control: an ostentatious opening, one that can't be opened and closed, sensually and cinematically, before a kiss.

Picture an ear closing sensually or cinematically before a kiss: it curls up, a flower rotting in slow motion, the cartilage white and amorphous.

So the ear is a little territory, a little death landscape, where radio signals are received, where love is received.

My father dies on a Tuesday. I go to Aarhus on the Wednesday. On Thursday night there's a seminar on Marguerite Duras in an artist workshop at Carlsberg in Copenhagen. I don't cancel, I say I'll attend by phone. I don't attend as a body, only as a voice.

In the days after his death, I pick up the phone once: When Marguerite Duras calls.

I'm thirty-two, I'm lying in my mother's bedroom with the spiral cord of the rotary phone around my wrist, a heavy bracelet, the way a bishop's robes and crown jewels and armatures with all their complexity give the wearer a sense of solidity.

Of authority.

I'm thirty-six, I've been on the phone for over ten years now. A slim red 80s phone, a grey rotary phone, an invisible ear plug, a vibration, whatever. Get off my phone! It's my phone! I say, and I say oh, why can't we talk again, don't leave me hanging on the telephone, come on, even though I'm in love, I don't dare call, but when would I ever dare call again? The telephonic is the machine that sets intimacy to the max and crumbles it just as fast. The phone: a thing, a concept, a transmitter, a form of thought, an awkward manmade object that makes it possible to imagine connections through time and space. The phone rings at 11pm. The phone rings when you look at it. The phone as a medium for the call of the past and the call into the future. The perfect memory machine, the perfect metaphor for all human relationships, all notions of love. I've fetishised the phone as an explosion of power and powerlessness, of clinging and distance, precisely because of the voice suspended in the receiver that paralyses and engulfs and interrupts. The phone as some rusty, antiquated hoarseness, but gorgeously whispering, it's just my brother calling, not a dead person, who was it anyway that called? Who? I've been obsessed with the idea of the technological as either elevated to a messianic life force, humanity's salvation, or stigmatised as something that fucks with originality, the voice as a cheap copy of what it is maybe supposed to be, whatever a voice is anyway. The voice on the phone: an eternally delayed edition of itself, an obscene facsimile, if I can be an obscene facsimile, there are no expectations, I can be as cheap and shameless as I want, the copy masturbates and has a hundred rubbery orgasms. I watch *Trollz* with my five-year-old daughter, a cartoon about coquettish troll girls, Ruby, Amethyst, Onyx and Topaz, they have *Spell Phones*, a riff on cell phones, *"Spell Calls" are used to cast spells on other Trollz across long distances. To initiate a Spell Call, the caller places a spell bead in the spell bead slot after reciting the incantation and then dialling the phone number of the intended recipient and hitting the cast button. The Spell Phone then transfers the spell through the phone line and when the recipient picks up the phone the spell is released through the receiver of the phone. It is a useful function that allows Trollz to cast spells across long distances, but a lot of teenagers misuse the function and instead use it to play pranks.* I'm that kind of prank caller. I'm a naughty phone addict. I watch Lady Gaga's *Telephone*: Gaga and Beyoncé in their awkward and flamboyant outfits. Gaga dances around a woman's prison with a giant, clunky Nokia 3310, I love it, the video is hyperaware of its own likely demise, in not so long, it'll look so crazy dated, in not so long, both their clothes and the giant flip phone will be so last year, we might as well turn it all up, we might as well be devoured by the phone's death-denying motherfucker of a ringtone.

Put your old interests to rest, my friend says.

The telephone is dead, long live the telephone!

Now it's ringing, Amalie is calling from the Duras seminar in Copenhagen! I pick up the grey rotary phone in my mother's bedroom and speak for four and a half minutes to an audience, I say:

In Marguerite Duras's film Le Navire Night, *a man and a woman have a love affair, but without ever meeting each other: they only speak to each other on the phone.*

In Le Navire Night, *two voices speak over an image of what at first looks like a wet heart, and then a glittering blood-red shirt. Black orgasm! they say.*

I can't write with the same authority as Duras. But I can let the uncompromising nature and rhythms of her films rub off on me.

I try to write like that, so that the text becomes a dynamic still-life. Passive, movable, plotless, exalted. Like when you make yourself come, alone, the room is dark, everything is still, in

your mind a crowd of bodies. I try to write so that every envi-
ronment becomes a mental image. The power flows from actors,
bodies and objects into the world, into the space of the text,
maybe outside the order of the text, and later it returns.

I try hard to write like that — I don't know whether I actually
succeed — so that all bodies can be linked together, can be
technologically extended into the external world. My charac-
ters are stylised, without any essence, but still active like the
characters in India Song *and maybe in* Le Navire Night: *ready*
for anything. In love. Present to an explosive space of possi-
bility, related to someone or something, but on the screen, we
see, robbed of the fiction of identity's coherence, incapable of
proving it.

I hang up.

There's light in the hallway.

The light is reflected in the picture frames above the laun-
dry basket. Johannes Ewald's powdered wig, the corners of
Jens Baggesen's mouth.

My mother's bedroom is full of shadows, a little bedside
lamp.

My essay on Duras is irritating, full of pathos.

A poster on the wall: a reproduction of a *stela* from Ancient
Egypt, Nefertiti and Akhenaton with their love hands extended to the Sun God. Stoic and engaged. I imagine love as
a telephonic, physical energy: the telephone voice is sucked
into the body, heightens the senses, afterwards a laid-bare
experience doled out like kisses.

I have a memory of looking at someone I'm in love with. My boyfriend is sleeping or temporarily disappeared into his own thoughts. I look at him. He snores, he's looking out of the window. Maybe it's before he's even my boyfriend. Maybe there are other bodies. Maybe I've already experienced this multiple times before. Maybe he and I have only just met, it's the Friday that we danced at a house party like wild monkeys, drunk on G&Ts, and ended up in his apartment and stayed in his bed for twenty-four hours, he's written me a letter with a red seal: he and I are Leonardo da Vinci and La Gioconda reincarnate, love is mythical. Or it's the weekend in London when I'm going to have a beer with him at a bar without really knowing what he looks like, he folds a yellow Post-It into a bird, we drink and talk, we've been sending frantic Facebook messages to each other all January. I move into his little room for three days. Or it's the afternoon he gets to Copenhagen, we haven't seen each other for months, we're anxious, his flight is delayed, maybe we won't get to see each other before I have to pick my daughter up from preschool, will we make it, will he close the door behind him before we've taken off our clothes, we're in love, out of breath and nervous, facing something new, but we still don't know what, we don't even know what we think about anything anymore, maybe we thought we didn't like twelve-tone music or denim jackets or parmesan cheese, but now we love it all, you could convince us of anything, you could get us to join a cult! Maybe I wake up during the night and see him right there, like a corpse, love stretched out in time, in the process of forcing entry into terrains usually sealed. I look at him, consider all the things that have kicked my feelings into high gear: the eyelashes, the skin, the hair, the lips, the shoulders, the fingers, the belly, the legs. I try to understand why I'm so smitten. Soon after he stirs, now there's movement, blood, like a phone being hung up. It's no longer possible to try to understand what love is.

And there isn't anything to say. The only thing someone in love can say is: *I adore you because you are adorable.*

You're so crazily adorable.

I don't get the chance to say this on the phone. The Duras seminar is over now. I didn't write more texts, I wasn't asked to give another reading. I didn't dare be the voice without a body for more than four and a half minutes. I have to go and check on my sleeping daughter, I have to go downstairs to have a cup of coffee with my mother and my older brother. I have the doubled sense of loneliness and alertness that I usually only feel after an event which, according to my own expectations, ought to activate the most epic feelings, but maybe for exactly that reason, because of the narrative pressure, for example, the bombastic nature of the end of life, the demand for an appropriately large emotional reaction, makes me apathetic, frenetically focused, but disoriented too, makes me want to do something else. Thoughts feel clear. Like they can be separated and put back together in new arrangements. Every desire can easily be analysed. I was restlessly rubbing my eyes, but now I'm looking without blinking. An image is drawn once again in the brain or on the wall: greasy eyeliner around the eyes. What did the ancient Egyptians do when they cried, and the sun just baked and baked, their cheeks must have been covered in the most incredible long black lines.

All epic feelings are as delayed as they are premature.

But I still hope that Marguerite will call again, even if it's from the soil under the cemetery in France, from the darkened page of a book. I want her to call me again so I can say more, come on, Marguerite, please sweetie, then I'll say this:

In Marguerite Duras's films, sound progressively becomes an expression of resistance to the power of the visual. That's how it is in Son nom de Venise dans Calcutta désert, *a film that reuses the entire soundtrack from Duras's earlier film,* India Song. *The soundtrack* to India Song *is already autonomous: voices and images are constantly out of sync. There's no illusion that the sound is coming from the images. And the voices are many, an entire chorus has their own chattering role in the narrative like guests at a party. The voices can discuss both past and future. Their gossip is the material of the film. But they have no bodies, and the bodies we actually see — the beautiful diplomat's wife, Anne-Marie Stretter, the various men she surrounds herself with — aren't attached to the voices of the choir.*

India Song's *images are interiors, and the story is set in French Indochina with France as the occupying power.* Son nom de Venise dans Calcutta désert's *visuals, on the other hand, are silent, one long shot of a ruined palace in Southern France, once owned by the Jewish Rothschild family, occupied by the Nazis during the war. Now France is the occupying power.* India Song *was filmed here too, in the palace, but the sets are long gone. The camera pans across the ruined rooms, a flickering lamp illuminates the rooms. We hear the voices and the soundtrack from* India Song *in the dark, between peeling paint and rubble; now the sound seems almost more alive.*

The power dynamics have shifted.

But also the power dynamics between image and text:

The image only takes its meaning from the text that slides across it. Duras wanted to destroy the medium of film as she had already destroyed the text, in the sense that her film, La Femme du Gange, *arose from the massacre of three books. Duras writes that herself somewhere — she wants to create a 'master image', a completely neutral image, the ultimate image.*

Maybe it's a clever trick — to use the same soundtrack, but create an overlay of countless visuals? By the end, we can't tell them apart, we have to let the images dissolve.

The film has risen from writing's grave. Now the film image is dying. Through the soundtrack, we've had the images' atmospheres inside us. Maybe we remember the images through sound. Now a new form of text is being resurrected, the sound as text. The always-agile sound that can't be beaten down.

The phone.

It's ringing.

It's ringing.

Four times.

HELLO, YEESSSSS!

Two voices speak over an image of what at first looks like a wet heart and then a glittering, blood-red shirt, they say:

(The voices, won't they be done soon. They're speaking with so much pathos, I can barely handle it.)

Now instead they say:

Your grief is ambiguous and defeated, but defiantly pompous. It's not uncommon, but not acceptable either (grief never is). Your grief is a kind of relief and then a kind of shame at the relief. Your grief is a little melancholic, a little pleasant, a little pleasing, you're ashamed of that too. Grief is about considering others who are grieving, who grieve differently and more intensely than you, imitating them or distancing yourself from them. Your grief feels insignificant, minimal, maybe it doesn't exist at all, you can't find it, you're stuck in many of its corners, you're searching, so can you please act a little like you're going to keep searching, can you feel anything, what if your body is a delay-machine. Grief is a negotiation of rituals, how they're supposed to be experienced and executed, the rituals are all the only thing, the feelings are still swelling inside you like nomadic, luxuriously wrapped gifts, completely out of step with what you know, what you think grief is, what you think time is, what you think life is, what you think annihilation is, what you think change is, what you think you've been told, did anyone actually teach you anything about this, you have no idea what you're supposed to do.

Grieve one so to be able to grieve the other.

Grieve your father's death to be able to grieve a broken family.

A catastrophe rarely comes alone, or at least there are only a few years between them, she says over coffee and crumb cake.

The music from the computer.

Robert Wyatt, that old crooner, don't you like it when Robert Wyatt sings?

There's no picture.

The frozen image disappeared too. Technical difficulties. If we can't see anything, what then?

I can't see you, are you there?

You're pixellated. Are you there?

You're frozen.

Are you home alone?

I love you.

Are you frozen?

Torpedo my hand into your pixels.

See you soon, Marguerite.

I can't remember when I last spoke to my father on the phone.

He wasn't so caught up in the family gossip and the good-byes, the little admonitions and shared recollections. Yes, I'm doing fine, I need to pack some warm clothes, no, is that right, wonderful, my train should be getting in around eleven, we've packed lunch, oh no, did she call, when's the last time you spoke to her, is she completely out of it, is it all bonkers over there, are you making Indonesian food or do you have that Ethiopian bread or coupons or pickled eggs, is there a cold front coming over Jutland, did L really turn ninety, why don't you come and visit, then we can do something nice, then you can get a little love and care, then I can see how you look, I haven't seen you in a while, see if your clothes look nice, is your hair decent, is your shirt wrinkled, is there hair on your skirt as usual, can we go out with you looking that way?

He wasn't like that.

So there was more room for everyone who loved the warmth
of the receiver.

Loved having a boiled lobster ear.

My dad didn't communicate like you're supposed to, or: in
the way that we wanted. My mother's communication is
central, it took up most of the space. It still is everything.
The listening and the speaking that a family ferments in.
My father's ears are flushed nevertheless, mostly in memories, in pictures too: the big red Dumbo ears; the dead body
we see is pale. The phone didn't warm him up. My mother and us and the red wine and vigour and the house with
all its contents, the feeling of the lake nearby, the garden
flora, the nightingale and books and the brain activity and
ping pong and countless people warmed him up, and later
when he couldn't walk anymore the little stereo system and
the rotating CDs and the chocolate and the television kept
him warm. And before that so many other things we barely
know about; like all people, he had his passions which we'll
never fully understand, everyone ought to have bards and
ghostwriters as followers, somebody to write down everything that happened. But we hope that we were the ones who
gave him the real warmth in his body. After his death, odd-
ly enough, we spend time wondering whether that was true.
We can't ask, even though we would never have asked, what
does that kind of question even sound like? How long does
he stay warm, how long does an ear boil after a pop song, a
phone call. How long do lobsters boil, crabs. How long do
jellyfish from Lillebælt boil in a pot before their bodies turn

to steam. How long does the glass screen stay warm after a long conversation. How does a voice end. Or: The voice is gone, the leg nerves are gone too, the head starts to go, the brain bulb has gone out, can we duck under the table, will the cane drop to the floor, are the Waldorfs already tucked into the salad, what happens when you buy a tame duck and rile it up? Will the gestures and food colouring be enough, the dance of the blackheads on the nose skin, the eyebrows moving up and down? Where do the woods end, how do the trees sway in the horizon, when do they fade? Who teaches a ten-year-old girl to sing in the woods, to sing on her bike? What makes a bike keep going when the legs don't work, who helps an old body up a hill so the body can sit on a bench and look out over the lake one last time, a son or a daughter or a wife or a seagull? How tough are the vocal chords, what do dandelions spit up, how long can skin hold the intestines together, how long can the brain handle the legs not obeying, how do you sow lettuce, when does the lettuce come out of the ground, tell me please. How do hedgehogs mate, now their quills are shaking, they're so cute, how do we get the hedgehogs out of the strawberry net, can they stay in there forever. How bored does Daisy Duck get when she's served for Christmas Dinner, how ecstatically do boneless herring dance on the Christmas table. How high is the bench above the surface of the lake, how long do we sit on the bench. Is this the last time we'll sit together on the bench, has he sat on the bench so many afternoons, will I ever sit alone on this bench, will I ever play the Donald Duck game by myself, will I ever watch for grebes alone, will I ever buy the silly ashtrays or the small porcelain garden gnomes for Christmas if not to give them to him, so my mother will shake her head noisily, secretly delighted by all that kitsch. Two mayflies are sitting on Robinson Crusoe, what does one say to the other, does it say see you on Friday, does it say see you on Saturday, when the shops are open late, does it say see you at the shop, see you on the bench, there are plastic bags of Tuborg Gold in the bushes, it says, tonight it's summertime, life is a little shorter, look at the summer night, there's a father and a daughter sitting on a bench, there's a mother and a father lying in two lounge chairs on the porch, there's a mosquito and a dragonfly sitting on an armrest, there's a bike lying in the grass on the way up the hill, what do they say to each other, they keep to the same rhythms, the trips keep to the same patterns, the bog lady is brewing over the lake, a smoke signal in East Jutland, see you on Sunday, how badly does the quiet one want to dance or die.

seventh call

Death is banal, I don't know if I can write anything about death at all. I don't have anything to say that hasn't already been said. And I don't know anything about death. Writing anything about death makes me feel really thick; postulating; cloddish.

I've never been near to death. I haven't flirted with death. I've never come close to it out of desperation or recklessness or decisiveness. I've seen my father and my grandmother: two natural deaths. *After a certain point, death is no longer about the single life lost. It's not even personal. It's what we are as a whole that qualifies us as targets.* A man from Afghanistan says in an interview that Danish people are so sensitive, they can't handle hearing about death, they start crying if they see a picture of a corpse. What hasn't he seen.

I imagine death as mild. Maybe it's not like that at all. Maybe the mildness has to do with the fact that everything is okay, or rather: that nothing is anything at all as soon as you're gone. To resign, to give yourself over to disappearance isn't painful. When I see a child's corpse on TV: She's not in pain. She's not suffering. She's not worried. The smallest and cutest ones don't worry about being gone any more than the heavy and awkward ones do.

On tate.org.uk I watch my English friend Elinor give a talk on *mirror touch*. *Mirror touch*, which could also be called *mirror-neuron synaesthesia* — is a state in which you, at the sight of another person being physically touched, experience the same tactile sensation. Your arm is stroked, I feel it on my skin. I cut my hand, you feel pain in your hand. A reflective grope. The ultimate empathic state, Elinor says. That we feel the same pain no matter how far-reaching it is. Mirror touch is about being in common. It is the exemplary sensory experience of being bound. Seeing and feeling across vast distances: Sight is no longer limited to the local. There are images everywhere that connect us outwards. The image's experiences land somewhere in our bodies. There are video recordings of executions, of kittens learning to balance and falling, of operations where bellies are opened and intestines pulled out like cables.

Everything we see. We haven't been able to imagine it. But then they've actually been there the whole time. I think about whether pain causes empathy or whether pain simply causes more pain. The notion that we all will die makes power struggles sink into gravel in our brains, how ridiculous are we!

Maybe it's not about having the ability to mirror-touch or not. Maybe mirror touch is more of a general condition: We're always a little porous and tender, there are plasters on the top of the fridge, Hello Kitty. We can't act like we don't know how much other parts of the world are hurting. We have mirrors in the strangest places, I raise an arm, you see your face in my armpit, I spread my legs, you see your mouth, you put your lips against the mirror, it feels cold, you exhale, a cloud of steam.

A body is lying there, what can it do? Not much. We look at it. We look with impolite, wide-open eyes. We can get away with it. We stare. The body doesn't need to fight to keep itself upright and moving anymore. It's not self-conscious. But still. We can't really take it. We can't handle that it's so quiet and painful here. Do you think the body is hungry? Should we have a dinner party? Should we set the lunch table? When will the lunch club guests be arriving? When are they coming to tumble around in food's life-giving power? Are all of the guests dead just like this body, will they all need to take off their corpse tunics first, be clean and naked? Should they put a little deodorant on? Pull a toothpick out? Tampon too? Now they're arriving, now they're arriving, shh, smooth the tablecloth, now they're sitting down at the table, they're filling their crystal glasses with Linie Aquavit, they're filling their beer mugs with Fynsk Forår. Look, the dead guests are eating, the dead are passing the rye bread basket around, they're letting the butter go around, the dead are eating egg salad, ham salad, chicken salad, the dead are eating glass noodles that slide down their oesophaguses, we can see right through the greyish tubes of their throats. The dead are spreading mustard on their pickles, which gleam yellowish like they're bedecked in a newborn's shit, the dead are piling their bread with fat and pickles and mustard. The dead are eating everything, down the hatch, I didn't know that they were capable of that, their finger skin is wrinkled, that's why their nails look like they're growing. The dead open packages of sausage, liver pâté, cheese, pastrami, horseradish, they rip the paper off the cheeses, they eat goats' cheese, Primadonna and brie, there's not enough food to go around at all. Their pace is unbelievable, they smack their lips, they eat all the shrimp, they dump red onions over their hair like flowers that have been standing too long, reeking over a coffin, and are just now letting their dark red leaves fall.

My father is dead. My mother opens the window in my father's room at the nursing home right away so something like a soul can fly out, as she says, maybe a little fictitious bird (the call from the nursing home came late, he's having trouble breathing, the nurse said, wheezing, you should get here as soon as you can; she steps out of the taxi at the entrance just as the last air in my father's lungs is driven out of his nostrils, maybe a fervid sound; she doesn't get to hear it, four minutes too late).

My mother, she can't study the body like the person in love studies their object of love, as if it were a corpse, with the expectation that movement will start up again in just a moment: this body won't be coming round again.

I think they were married for forty-nine years.

I like that she opened the window. I like the ritual, whatever it means, it doesn't mean anything other than: She acknowledges that he is dead, she manages to weave the ritual into her grief, the sweetness of the open window has a calming effect on me.

It's not common practice anymore to open the window so the soul can leave the room. It's not because we've given up the soul entirely: We like to imagine it as ethereal, as enchanted and animated, a foreign being inside us, some kind of vibrating engine, it's already all around us, I think, and in our relationships. We call the soul X, the window is opened, nothing happens. We look at the dead body; nothing flies out. X is already in the radio waves and in the wireless network. X doesn't need to be atomised and ascend because X never really had a form, never cast an anchor. X was never an enigmatic lump inside us, X was never an arcane definition of who we are at heart when everything has been peeled away; X was never a pattern we kept using to make decisions, as if we were one big indisputable repetition of ourselves; X was never a patronising authority over our otherwise dutiful curves; X was never the white lady's lovely body; X is maybe rather a goosebump body; X is maybe feathers tickling an intravenous, winged stab in the gut; X is maybe a cluster of feelings inside us; X is maybe an engine; X is maybe the ability to leave something, the ability to get closer to something else; X is maybe that we sometimes bring others inside us and sometimes are brought into others; X is maybe that we'd never be able to let each other's consciousness be; X is maybe the borders inside us, that they're always shifting; X is maybe that the borders already contain the catastrophe; X is maybe the nonhuman inside us; X is maybe the feeling of the corpse as a friendly presence inside us from the day we are born; X is maybe what that feeling makes us think and do.

Or maybe my mother opens the window so the cadaver itself can look out with the last remains of warmth inside it. My father's hands are cold when I touch them the day after his death. Maybe his intestines are lukewarm. Maybe they're still boiling, like piss on a cold day. I read about *necropolitics* and *necroaesthetics*: the latter a state between living and death where the body is still warm. A haunting state where the limbs are loose, sit differently, where the body appears foreign and uncanny, where intimacy is broken, flesh is distinct, at least it's still there. The dead messes with time and has the ability to intervene in the world of the living: the corpse lies there and speaks to us. In William Faulkner's *As I Lay Dying*, Addie dies; while she waits for death, she is referred to in the past tense, but after her death the sons and widower talk about her in the present. On a chaotic journey, the corpse is hauled though the south, the trip takes way too long, the hearse rattles along. Addie is about to rot right down, and she forgets to stay dead after her death, she starts talking, in the novel she even has her own monologue.

My father doesn't start talking. Maybe we're disappointed, but he was also just a Danish teacher, and Addie is a literary heroine after all. We wait in the room at the nursing home for a while. The undertaker arrives with his slow, overly polite talk. I don't want to cry, maybe because my mother is crying and trying to stop crying and keeps apologising. I make an effort not to, once I start, it'll be the kind of crying where I won't be able to stop. Who else would I be able to cry in front of if not my mother and my brother and my daughter? But I definitely don't want to cry in front of them. I only start crying when the coffin is opened during the ceremony in my mother's house, then it's okay, then all of the pathetic — but still internal and unsettling — sniffling won't offend anyone. The coffin is opened: it's been almost four days since death arrived. Thanatos, Freud's concept of the death drive, describes the human desire to throw yourself into sadistic and self-destructive situations. Thanatos is a craving to return to an inorganic, lifeless state, an ideal *nothingness*. The lid of the coffin flies off, and calm spreads. But in a necroaesthetic room I imagine the world of the dead is corporeal. Death is not a quiet, clean space. Death is above all not mild and natural, but violent, ugly and mute because we know that the cadaver will soon begin to rot. And the corpse wants to expound on that! In all its vulgar talk! As soon as the lid flies off, the cadaver opens its mouth and blabbers away with its yellowish teeth and whitish tongue, recounting in an ethical spurt all the invisible and quiet forms of death that exist in the world, their raving ugliness and absurdity: that's the clammy, vibrating-with-worms mission of the soon-to-be disintegrated corpse. But I don't want to listen to all that horror right now, even though one death says something about everyone's deaths; I don't even want to listen to my father, even if he suddenly started to say something, it would feel historical, almost like a voice on an old cassette, a radio broadcast from the 1940s, it's been that long since I actually heard him rant in that excited rabble-rousing way; that was before he got sick. Instead I want to stay in that room: the flowers by the coffin, my daughter running around, she bumps into the white coffin lid propped against the bookshelves, imagine if the lid fell onto the corpse, would it get a bruise, would there be a scene, would it be in line with my father's existential Twister aura, his fifteen thumbs, my twenty, the food has been delivered and the Muscatel poured, isn't it about time something went wrong, are we actually having a nice time, do we almost love that everything is so normal, are we this happy to see each other, are the festivities really that much in my father's spirit, are we celebrating his life to grasp his death with the looming danger of slapstick scenes, that the coffin for instance doesn't make it through the door, that the lid pops off, and the body rolls into the bed of roses, that the coffin follows, that the animals crawl into the cosy, padded compartment to hibernate, that the corpse is blanketed by frost and snow until spring arrives, that it thaws then, quietly marinating in pollen, and smells so warm and soft that the hedgehogs curl into quill balls, that they give birth to their young there, and then it's autumn, fallen apples plant themselves like beautiful red-brown balls in his armpits, waistband, eye sockets, and become an acidic squished copper-brown covering over what's half-disappeared by now, and then it's winter, a year has passed. The funeral is an occasion to remember. I want to share anecdotes from my father's life, but I can't remember a single one without the feeling that I've forgotten something important. My mum can. The stories are mostly hers, she's the narrator. My parents' lives run parallel to each other, but it's mostly thanks to my mother that we've been able to listen to the living, shall we give it a try?

I'm thirty-six, I'm watching *Her Master's Voice*. The British Nina Conti is a ventriloquist. Her former lover and teacher in the art of ventriloquism, Ken Campbell, is dead. Nina has inherited his dolls, including the little monkey, MONKEY. Nina doesn't know what to do with all the dolls. She takes a trip to Vent Haven in Kentucky. Here you can 'bury' old ventriloquist dolls, put them on display: all the dolls together! You look across the room: unsettling, like an outlandish dining room in a nursing home. Nina never told Ken how much she loved him, never thanked him for teaching her ventriloquism. She was young when they were together, he much older. She was always saying the wrong thing, she felt dumb while he shone. She felt that she didn't give him anything in return. It's touching when Nina films herself in multiple scenes in her hotel room, trashy and melancholy in bed, with the dolls by her side, occasionally the big Ken Campbell doll with the grey hair and the funny teeth, but mostly the monkey. The monkey gets all the provocative lines; it's only when the monkey is speaking for Nina that things are said unfiltered. Nina misses Ken, and the monkey responds by accusing her of 'psychic necrophilia'; the pretty girl Nina would never have that kind of language in her mouth. I don't think that Nina experiences the monkey's voice as her own. I think she imagines it as an interlocutor, a titillating version of herself, a new perspective, something alien. Ventriloquism draws a rift between the self and self's body, ventriloquism is an ideal way to understand what happens when you're working with a first-person narrator, a figure that can't, in any sense, be pure, but only act as an assemblage of foreign voices, syntaxes, rhythms, vocabularies, of sentences stolen and mimed and downloaded and sampled from thousands of bodies and texts and sources and mouths, voices laid inside us from the outside, a machinery inside us.

But ventriloquism is also an exemplary way, here at any rate, to understand a version of love that seems strange to me at first: Because how can Nina, who is married — you see her husband in the kitchen, he looks cute — long so much for someone else. Here, love is a longing for the dead with all the loss and the regret that comes with it. Here, love is doubled. Love can exist in multiple parallel forms, just like how the weathered tenderness I feel for the boyfriend I've known for many years exists alongside my being in love with the person I've just met.

Actually, we don't have access to Nina's loss. In the conversation with the monkey, her loss become something collective. The little fabric doll around Nina's hand opens into the shy Nina's brain. Language tumbles out of the monkey's mouth.

eighth call

The computer is on. Nina and the Ken doll are speaking in

the night-time darkness.

I sit on the sofa and listen to the film's voices. There's almost no light in the living room. The voices come towards me. My stomach rumbles. My intestines are singing *Eternal Flame*, they want to go out and play.

The language of the intestines is just more frank.

The Muscatel is gone, my father's ashes have been strewn. I've had my second child, published four books, and later: a broken nuclear family, a kind of breakdown. But here I am: still in the death space, attached to the idea of the corpse and decay as a tool for thinking, a frivolous abstraction. My intestines say, give us a break. Instead become better friends with the idea of the corpse *inside you*. It doesn't have anything to do with you. It doesn't belong to you. It's not about *your* death. Death isn't just dying or experiencing someone else die, but ways of dying in themselves. *I repeat that death is behind us. Death is the event that has always already taken place at the level of consciousness.* My intestines, knotted, out of breath, speak: death is millions of ways to die, death as illness: anorexia, cancer, poisoning, wear; death as vulnerability: natural disasters, invasions, terror, airstrikes, ash clouds, falls from skyscraper windows, landmines – a given, but not an end. Drones fly across a landscape, a thousand children fall, a thousand children know they will fall too, a thousand children press their fingers into soft cheeks to feel their skulls. Death is taking over. Instead of disciplining our lives, power turns our vulnerability up and down, decides whether we'll be discarded soon. Death doesn't end, it's always in process, just like all conversations: you were already working on dying before the phone rang, you're already working on dying even in your most radiant and chattering moment.

I go to the bathroom to take a death selfie, I don't know how *I'm dead and I'm going to die and I'm dying and I'm dying right now and oh hold my hand now oh take my bones in yours oh let's make out*, my selfie should include my intestines, it should include my ribcage, my gold eye shadow, my best quarter profile, the stretch marks, the tongue and my X. I store the image on a cloud, the last bastion of the undead. I want far too much. My fingers are wet and drop the phone on the hard bathroom floor. The corpse inside me is like a friendly, patient rubber woman, I lean into her, out of her, and later —

4.
FRIDAY NIGHT

FRIDAY NIGHT.

B and Q lazily side by side on the sofa.

Their skins are detachable.

Their skins, they get taken off and put on like surgical scrubs or custodial uniforms, they're so practical.

Right now B and Q are wearing them.

They like to be civilised.

B and Q, they live in the same house. A cafetière, a bank account and Æ's snores. Occasionally there's contact, occasionally their skins sink into each other, then they tear themselves loose again.

Suddenly the sofa fabric rips. The padding pops out, the cushions split in half, the cake plates shatter in B and Q's hands, the almond cake crumbs drift in the air around them.

The floor under the sofa has opened — in the middle of the floorboards, a hole whose thick splinters poke into its middle: a stabbing openness.

B's body slides down.

Q's body slides down.

B and Q haven't drunk any elixir to become small, any elixir to become large again; this isn't a fairy tale.

It's like their bodies haven't gone through any changes: they slide down through the floor with the same knees and cheeks and the same familiar methods of adjusting their bodily sensations.

It's strange but comforting to experience something completely new: that her body is still the same, B thinks.

As if her experiences don't have any effect on her body.

As if her body will just keep going no matter the gravity of the situation. As if her skin is suddenly smeared with adrenaline and hardens. So that she can breastfeed in a sweet state of intoxication, while her gut is in a second dimension: inflamed and swollen.

Where should we go? Q asks.

I think we should go down to the underworld, B says.

I must have invited the two of us down here.

We were so wet and horny between the broken porcelain plates.

I was trying to imagine what death is. Friday night was moving so slow that it almost stalled out.

We're about to go down into an apocalypse.

You can imagine that it's our own.

This is not a romance. We're not Orpheus and Eurydice. Orpheus is gay and loves the director, Eurydice is getting off work soon and wants to go home to her boyfriend.

Are you keeping up? If the two of us are going under, we have to do it together.

You can be: a jerk. My betrothed. Someone I play with.

It'll start like a waltz in cream, maybe it'll end in a thousand pieces, or as the start of an accelerated thought.

Come on come on!

Q's in, so they've made it down. B thought they would follow a dark ravine, a narrowed path. That maybe they had to go through the white man's apocalypse, the kind of disaster where everything is an open field, overgrown, a group of denim-clad men with pocketknives show them how to cook a rat over a fire, suck the meat from the tail, but B and Q are suddenly in a very expansive space. They jump into an organic fantasy: on the horizon, fields, tomato plants and pink sky. They jump over a jellied bog, their wellies sink into the greenish mass and pop up again with a squelch, like someone pulling their dentures out of their gums again and again.

They trudge through yellowish grass with boggy patches and finally: a glistening black house atop a hill.

The glistening: rot has set in.

B and Q hold hands, but not as lovers anymore, now like small eager schoolchildren.

Passionless allies.

A quivering sheen on the black woodwork. The planks aren't hard at all. They've softened as if they've been underwater for a long time. Screws sit loosely in the wood covered by mussels and miniature glass eyes and yo-yos and pink finger rings.

Now it's obvious: The black colour has masked the house's jelly consistency, but now the house is showing its discomfort.

B and Q try to look inside, they put their hands through the open windows.

The house doesn't just wobble. A wild sound streams out of the living room, that's why it's shaking.

Someone playing ARGH ARGH ARGH.

Someone playing LOVECOCK.

Someone playing HELL YEAH.

Someone playing A NOISY PSYCHOTIC SOUND OUT OF PROPORTION.

B and Q can feel the sound with their hands now.

Like the wind of a mad hairdryer on the fingertips.

But before B and Q can figure out what the sound is, they realise that for now it has simply led them to the house and made them look through the windows.

When B and Q's eyes have adjusted to the slimy darkness, they make out the outlines of a crowd of dollish bodies inside.

Maybe the dollish bodies are like this:

They're lying on the floor or sitting cross-legged or with their legs back in an exaggeratedly athletic pose. They're hanging from the ceiling with one leg. They're rising in geometric formations. They do as they like: maybe they're loafing around. A striped cat stalks slowly from embrace to embrace. Hands take turns holding the cat's mouth as if to turn its meow into an old-fashioned whistle, the kind that kids send each other from one tree house to the next.

The dollish bodies aren't real, but a *show*: a first-world-problem performance of the space that exists between being powerless and totally dead, made of glass fibres, made of foam rubber, made of papier-mâché, made of plasma, made of owl vomit, made of oatmeal balls, duck fat.

B and Q have moved away from the house.

They've kept walking without realising it.

Almost in step.

They walk side by side through something that could be a bog squelching away.

Mud far up their legs, like Æ's shit, but more shapeless, therefore more unsettling.

I think we're about to reach the edge of the crazy sound! B says.

I think we'll be okay! B says.

What would Æ say about this? Q asks.

Æ.

B and Æ were on their way home from the playground, Æ said: I would like some of those sweeties that look like dummies when we get home.

And then she made her first comparative analysis of the two Disney movies she had seen again and again.

Is it right that Rapunzel is sitting in the tower and can't get out, and that Elsa in *Frozen* can't get out of her room either?

That's true, honey, that's how it is, B says.

And listen to this, in *Snow White* and *Sleeping Beauty* and *Beauty and the Beast* too, the women are locked away.

By themselves or someone else.

Just like in Charlotte Brontë's *Jane Eyre*, where the 'mad' wife sits in her room in the attic, going crazy.

Does the attic make her mad, or was she already that way?

And then there are all of the basements around the world, full of women.

And all the basements of the brain.

Of course B says all of that too fast for Æ to understand, her way of talking is to herself, an exercise in teaching Æ to think.

Maybe Æ picks up the nuances, that's what her brain can do — growing rampant, no one knows what she doesn't understand.

Æ, eyes rolling in her head, her hair is about to take off and torpedo the sky, B thinks about her when she goes to the Biennale in Venice.

B enters the American Pavilion at the Biennale in Venice. Joan Jonas in the American Pavilion, a large installation with multiple films projected onto free-standing screens. The main characters in the films are girls.

Angelic girls in white dresses and white headbands and with childish gestures. They wave long coloured ribbons. They hold round pieces of cardboard in front of the camera. On the cardboard, film projections of beehives, teeming bee bodies. It's a swarm!

Images of dinosaurs are projected onto a chalkboard: The girls draw the dinosaurs' bodies with chalk, fumbling as they try to frame their outlines. You can tell they're children: they can't draw that well in reality. Now they're trying to do their best and be more grown-up than they are.

The way that these children aren't children, but props of grace and focused intelligence. The children's slow charm put into play by their clumsy hand gestures.

B watches a film by Peggy Ahwesh, *Martina's Playhouse*, on ubuweb:

Martina is talking to the camera, she's a little girl, but not a baby, she's just playing that she is a baby.

She lies on the floor of her mother's living room with all of the toys and tells the camera that she wants to wear a nappy.

Her voice is so cute.

She's caught up in the game, the camera is a character in the game, she chatters and talks and wants a nappy and her legs in the air.

In another room the mother's friend, much more self-aware. She's familiar with the camera and knows what it means to be seen, she's nervous.

B thinks:

Can little girls be themselves?

Just be allowed to do things, to want it all, in the bizarre mess that wraps around a life?

Sitting in the middle of a room with props and dolls without lower bodies or legs and old dress-up clothes and sequinned blankets and half-eaten poppyseed rolls and dirty Disney leggings.

Mum tells her guests stories about friends and money and her worries.

About mum's mess.

About mum's flip-flopping feelings.

Unclean and unworthy and always riled up about something.

Mum wants it all!

Smoking cigarettes small and hollow.

Vacuuming and going out.

Writing and producing and thinking.

Drinking coffee, tea, water, Campari, whiskey, wine, beer, fruit juice, cola.

Doing nothing.

Doing everything.

Loving and not loving.

Leaving her boyfriend and not leaving her boyfriend.

Fucking a thousand strange men and women, not fucking them.

Resisting injustice and enduring injustice a little longer.

Sleeping in a tight embrace with the kids every night, occasionally not sleeping with them there at all.

With Mum in the garden, balancing a tray, a stuffed tote bag, holding the gate open, all the cups and the milk and the coffee and the nectarines and the grapes and the sunglasses and the sugar and the sparkling water and the cake and the little Quality Street chocolates and the toys and the books and the markers and the colouring books and the notebooks and sitting on a blanket, bum wet from the grass.

Æ finds snails, makes them race, one in each hand and up the arm, then down on the grass with them. They slime their own ways, so slowly, but still as if they're racing away:

the illusory brown shells and the grey bodies that swiftly contract.

What do snails really want — they steer aimlessly away without going anywhere. An explosion of snails everywhere, a dispersal.

Where are they going, Mummy, Æ asks.

Who will they confuse, Mummy, Æ asks.

Who has power over them, Mummy, Æ asks.

Who are they trying to overthrow, Mummy, Æ asks.

Maybe it's not at all necessary to be able to think to be able to survive, Mummy, Æ says.

Maybe our consciousness, our brains aren't important in that way at all, Mummy, Æ says.

Maybe instinct isn't thinking at all, Mummy, Æ says.

Existence might be something completely different, Mummy, Æ says.

And then our passing doesn't mean so much, Mummy, Æ says.

Then it doesn't really matter that you make a mess.

That it's messy in your head.

That there isn't any order in mine either.

She doesn't say that, but that's how she is: gives her dolls desires, lets them have opinions. B would never give so much power to a doll.

B doesn't think that much independent life into a plant's or a rock's body.

B listens.

She wants to hear more.

B can't ask Æ for more words, or else there won't be any more.

The cautiousness.

B feels lucky when the light is finally off, when she is lying next to Æ in the double bed and they are suddenly talking. It's the intimacy she's been longing for all day.

Æ asked: If you die and go to the museum, Mummy, like the Grauballe Man, then can I just call you there if your phone isn't dead too, is it dead?

No, I'm afraid you can't, honey, B answered.

Because I'm not taking my phone.

And you can't call anyone else who's dead either.

You can't call the people lying in a mass grave in Mexico, plastic bags stuffed with bodies, four heads and sixteen torsos, a single hand. Refugees from the border without identification papers, hastily thrown into a pile by the border guards so they don't take up too much space, so you don't have to spend time locating their families. Now they're being dug up by the authorities, there are articles written and photos taken. The shovel is pleasantly cool, and the earth is completely black, it's night-time, there are lamps on the helmets, if you hold your hand close to the light, it'll get so warm.

You can't call the girl who is floating in the Mediterranean in the furious heat either, dressed in her pink leggings and polka-dot skirt, she is floating face down, in the sun, in the pleasant sun's warmth, so bright now after the cold of the night, her life raft sunk and her family drowned.

Her clothes are just like yours, and in that sense she seems to be alive still. Her clothes are like a fantastically decorated funeral procession. Colourful patches stuck to the blue surface of the sea. Slowly drifting toward land.

You can't call the dead in those Victorian photographs either, standing with a wooden trestle hidden behind them to hold their bodies upright, dressed to the nines in black taffeta dresses, lace aprons, jackets and waistcoats.

The trestle sticks awkwardly out behind their bodies, clumsy and amorphous. Like an extra leg that's only able to grow out once you've kicked the bucket.

As if a body on its deathbed were spliced with something else, like the man and the insect in *The Fly*.

Sometimes the dead stand with their living family members, stiff like a mannequin with open eyes, the living look all stiff in the eyes too.

Sometimes you can't see who is dead and who's alive: for example, the dead holding onto the waist of the living, a dead hand on the taffeta skirt of the living.

B thinks:

Sometimes she can't tell who is dead and who is alive.

A picture in an article about the organ trade: the stitches down a girl corpse's chest. But she looks like a cute little Frankenstein's monster. Something from a cartoon.

Æ has fallen asleep. She sleeps on her belly, round and compact, in her red-striped undershirt, with her teddy bear squashed against her chest and her cheek.

B and Q run.

They run through the mud, grunting like tractors frantically grinding through farmland.

LOVECOCK in and out of penis heads, cotton buds in and out of eyeballs.

ARGH ARGH ARGH in their innermost crucible.

HELL YEAH smeared across the landscape.

B asks:

Can a beautiful death performance be all for nothing?

Moving at max velocity, dissolved duck fat flaps in and slathers death into my bone marrow so I can only imagine that it's already taking place inside me. That I am just as dead as all of those who look dead, and all of those who look alive.

My corpse and I can run away together, hide out and eat cake, B says.

You and I can take our skins off, B says.

You and I can stage our own apocalypse, B says.

What's happening in the brains of those dollish bodies? Q asks.

Maybe it's like this? Q asks:

In their brains are small tea sets and dollhouses and sunsets and layer cakes and shovels of snow and buttercups and green doors and German shepherds and ravines and woods and hands with nail beds frayed from too much nature.

Or maybe it's like this?:

In their brains there's caring for their families, dreams of their home towns, their primary schools, dogs and cats playing in the gravel, the memory of their first kiss, missing their children's embraces.

Or maybe it's like this?:

In their brains is some dynamite from another galaxy and the courage we haven't yet felt, neither in ourselves nor in anyone else.

Or maybe it's like this?:

In their brains, it sounds like eighty old boomboxes playing. We don't understand how they communicate with each
other: hand gestures, bobbing eyebrows, long trails of bread
crumbs. Dust in the air floating through their feathery hair.

Or maybe it's like this?:

They want to throw their language out there, it's their revolt.
They say: See if you can hear us. They say: We don't have any
stable idea of how anything is. They say: We're affectionate
fools, we don't have any filter. They say: We're, like, so dead.
We've never felt closer to each other. That's the best way to
let off some steam.

Q starts running. Mud from his snakeskin heel shoots into
B's face, she gears up.

B runs behind Q.

She can't catch him.

She can still feel the warmth of his body.

Her hand slips into an air glove, warm, full of her own bones.

Above:

Drones like paper garlands.

Drone pilots in their dry and secure enclosures eliminate
the small white *bugs* crawling on their screens with the push
of a button.

What if that bug was Æ's face, B thinks.

What if it was my face.

What if it was my arse.

What if it was Æ's face tattooed across my bum cheeks.

What if it was all the little girls' faces tattooed across my bum cheeks.

Spanking square bums.

Spanking rhombus bums.

Spanking heart-shaped bums.

Spanking pixellated bums.

Spanking the outline of a thousand bums.

ACKNOWLEDGEMENTS

p. 83: the messages *'Listen, the bird paints with its fingers, twice. I repeat...* and then it repeats. Or: *Silence moves faster when it is played in reverse. Listen, twice'* draw on Tom McCarthy recalling Jean Cocteau's *Orphée* in 'An Interview with Tom McCarthy' by Mark Alizart, *The Believer,* 1 June 2008.

p. 116: the words *'After a certain point, death is no longer about the single life lost. It's not even personal. It's what we are as a whole that qualifies us as targets'* stem from *In the Future They Ate from the Finest Porcelain* (2016), directed by Larissa Sansour and Søren Lind.

p. 125: *'I repeat that death is behind us. Death is the event that has always already taken place at the level of consciousness'* is a direct citation from Rosi Braidotti's *The Posthuman* (Cambridge: Polity Press, 2013), p. 133.

BIOGRAPHIES

IDA MARIE HEDE (b. 1980) is the author of eight books and numerous plays. She holds an MA in Art History from the University of Copenhagen and Goldsmiths and graduated from the Danish Academy of Creative Writing in 2008. She has received the Danish Art Foundation's prestigious three-year working grant, and in 2018 *Bedårende* was nominated for the Danish Critics' Prize for Literature.

SHERILYN NICOLETTE HELLBERG has published translations of Jonas Eika, Johanne Bille, Tove Ditlevsen, and Olga Ravn, and holds a PhD in Comparative Literature from the University of California, Berkeley. In 2018, she received an American-Scandinavian Foundation Award for her translation of Caspar Eric's *Nike.*

Graphic design by Chloe Scheffe
Typeset in Media77 and Fugue
Printed and bound by KOPA, 2021

This publication was made possible through the support of the Jan Michalski
Foundation, the Danish Arts Foundation, and the Konsul George Jorck & Hustru
Emma Jorck's Fond

 **FONDATION JAN MICHALSKI POUR L'ECRITURE ET LA LITTERATURE**   Danish Arts Foundation   KONSUL GEORGE JORCK OG HUSTRU EMMA JORCK'S FOND

A CIP catalogue record for this book is available from the British Library
ISBN 978-1-9999928-9-7

Lolli Editions
132 Defoe House, Barbican
London EC2Y 8ND
United Kingdom
www.lollieditions.com